CW01373327

WHAT WE OWE THE DEAD

An experimental detective novel
set in a dystopian society

STEFANO GUALENI

Stefano Gualeni (Ph.D.) is an academic and author of philosophical reveries. He is a Full Professor at the Institute of Digital Games (University of Malta) and a Visiting Professor at the Laguna College of Art and Design (LCAD) in Laguna Beach, California.

Among his monographic books are *Virtual Worlds as Philosophical Tools* (Palgrave, 2015), *Virtual Existentialism* (Palgrave, 2020 – with Daniel Vella), *Fictional Games: A Philosophy of Worldbuilding and Imaginary Play* (Bloomsbury, 2022 – with Riccardo Fassone), and *The Clouds: An Experiment in Theory-Fiction* (Routledge, 2023).

https://gua-le-ni.com

(PAG. 02)
PART 1
ELEVII

(PAG. 184)
PART 2
GRACE

(PAG. 194)
PART 3
STEFANO

PART 1

ELEVII

<NOTE> Re-reading the whole thing again a few days after having returned to Sector 78, I realize a lot of work remains to be done on this draft. Likely because of my decision to move blocks of text over from my personal log, the tone of the document is occasionally too informal for an official report, and there are still unnecessary details and tangents that need to be abridged or excised entirely in the official submission.

All the interactions with Captain Kutta can be removed, and I should shorten the automatically generated text segments... as well as the document in general. I also need to make sure to remove the information I agreed to omit, as well as all the notes, including this one, after they have been addressed. </NOTE>

INVESTIGATION DAY 1

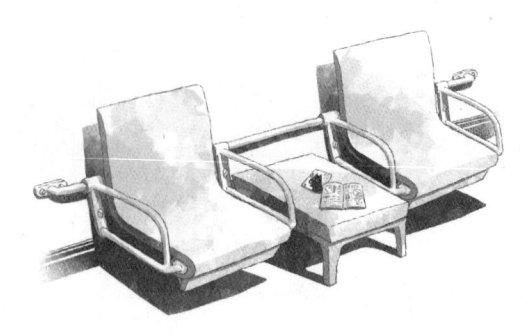

August 23 – SS8C

My introductory meeting with the head of the security station, Major Hestia Azucena, lasted less than half an hour. ~~She simply went through the same material I had received as part of my briefing five days prior. The chief was painstakingly thorough in her debriefing but added nothing to what I already knew from everything I had seen and read about the case. To her credit, she is very personable, and she did try to make me feel welcome. She even used the word "grateful" in relation to my having accepted this temporary transfer to her station. Twice.~~

Earlier the same morning, a staff member from the Surveillance Office had given me a brief tour of Station 8C, printed a new badge for me, and made sure my terminal was able to access station services and database information at the level of clearance specified on the aforementioned badge. With all the formalities out of the way, and with me already having met with the station chief, there was only one last onboarding procedure that needed to be sorted out: a station representative was to escort me to my new office. It was protocol, and, following protocol, the onus fell to Major Azucena herself, ~~who carried this out right after our somewhat disappointing meeting.~~

~~We took a short and silent walk along a corridor to an internal elevator. I was unable to tell whether the chief's aloofness was due to social awkwardness or whether she considered my presence a matter delicate enough to warrant discretion. In any case, once the elevator doors closed behind us, Major Azucena~~ smiled and ~~told me I should not hesitate to ask her directly for whatever I needed—either for my comfort or for the sake of the investigation. I took the major at her word almost immediately.~~ We were still on the elevator ride downtower when I inquired about whether Station 8C could spare a cyborg to assist me. With another smile, she informed me that Special Unit Deputy Bakola had already been briefed on the investigation and that they were eager to provide support.

The elevator doors opened with a hiss, revealing a part of the security station that had not been included in my morning tour. ~~Granted, there was little to see—the area's plain white walls and purposefully unremarkable decor would make it an unattractive destination for visitors. I wondered if me having to perform my duties in a tucked-away corner of the station was the result of a deliberate decision by Azucena. Had management made the conscious decision to separate me (and my case) from the rest of the staff? As unexceptional as they might have been,~~ The three rooms making up the area of Station 8C designated as "Floor B" merit special attention in this report, as the entirety of my investigative work took place here.

SS8C-B0

The elevator opened to B0, a relatively large, windowless

room with an elongated floorplan that was rectangular in shape. Bolted to the wall facing the elevator doors was a bench of the kind often found in waiting rooms. This model could fit up to three modular seats bolted to a shared, wall-mounted horizontal support, but this unit instead had a small postplastic table where the middle seat could have been. On top of the table lay two publications: the July issue of a specialized magazine called *Cond-Passion* and an illustrated tale for children. ~~I was unsure about what a cautionary tale for children was doing in a police station. The book happened to be one I had read many years ago, a sort of moral parable where a small act of neglect sets up a sequence of events with escalating consequences. If memory serves, it begins with a little boy forgetting to feed his dog and ends with the collapse of an interplanetary civilization.~~

Aside from the elevator entrance, Room B0 had two metal doors, one on each side of the bench—Room B1 on the left and Room B2 on the right. ~~The names of the rooms were painted in dark, sharp-cornered characters on the wall beside each door.~~ Precariously clinging to the smooth surface of the door to Room B1 was a tourist flyer meant for people visiting this cooling megatower for the first time. It was a common type of flyer that presented a stylized front view of HOOS-MING ONE, along with textual descriptions of various places of interest inside.

<NOTE> I took a picture of the flyer. Someone had drawn doodles on it with a marker, so these are not part of the original print. </NOTE>

The far end of this transitional space featured a kitchenette and two vending machines. There did not seem to be any cameras monitoring Room B0. ~~I meant to ask Major Azucena the reason for that but decided not to, as she seemed eager to fulfill her duty as a host and station representative as quickly as possible so that she could move on with the rest of her day.~~

HOOS-MING ONE
Antarctica's first!
13 km
Seed vaults
10 km
EXPLORE THE ORIGINAL SYPHON-MEGATOWER!
5 km
Alien wreck
Bird sanctuaries
HERE
Fields

SS8C-B2

~~While I was photographing the flyer in the main hall, the chief unlocked the door to Room B2 using her wrist badge. Unlike B0,~~ Room B2 was airy and naturally lit: the wall opposite the entrance consisted entirely of thick glass panels going from the floor to the ceiling. A heavy-looking metal table occupied the center of the space, surrounded by five matching chairs.

Major Azucena informed me that Room B2 was fully soundproofed and electro-magnetically screened, qualities that made it particularly suitable for formal depositions and interviews. ~~Someone with less tact would probably have referred to this as an "interrogation room."~~ The chief also specified that B2 had been reserved for my case, meaning that I had exclusive access to it until the end of my investigation. She then directed my attention to two ceiling-mounted cameras, adding that, whenever possible, security staff in Station 8C have a Special Unit in attendance during depositions. She explained that, in addition to being desirable for the safety of the officers, the recordings produced by the Special Units offered an additional point of view on the conversation that could also serve as a redundancy—~~in the engineering sense, which is to say~~ the duplicate of a critical function—in case of technical issues with the room's equipment. ~~I shared with the major that, depending on availability, we have the same policy uptower.~~

Although Room B2 was set up specifically to enable multiple methods of recording interactions with a subject, the chief emphasized that I was not obliged to take that extra measure and that how to use the space was entirely up to me. In fact, she added, I could even make Room B2 my office during the investigation if I thought that would facilitate my job.

~~As she was going into detail on some aspect of the recently upgraded electromagnetic screening, I walked to the glass wall facing the central syphon of HOOS-MING ONE. The view was astounding. From where I stood, I could also see a couple of bird sanctuaries hanging from various parts~~

~~of the tower structure by means of thick, padded cables. I had never seen a sanctuary in person before. Shrubs and succulent plants grew on their upper surfaces. On the top side of these artificial, floating islands were tree-like devices that were evidently designed to invite perching behavior. Looking upward, I could see another sanctuary suspended above. Its curved bottom surface was dotted with artificial tunnels and cave-like hollows from which swallows kept coming and going. I learned in school that the birds hid in these caves during the hottest hours of the day.~~

<NOTE> I must have spent the better part of a minute gawking, transfixed, at swallows darting back and forth around their floating islands. In an attempt to regain my attention, Major Azucena noted that sharing the tower with the birds was among the benefits of working close to the base of HOOS-MING ONE. I still could not believe I had a window all to myself. </NOTE>

~~On my way out of Room B2, I also noticed a small metal table in a corner. Resting on it was an empty pitcher and a stack of five upside-down postplastic glasses, all belonging to the same lime green set.~~

Major Azucena had just locked the door to the interview room behind us when the elevator doors hissed opened once again. In front of us, in the open space of B0, was the unmistakable crab-like body of a Special Unit. ~~Their angular shell and six pointy legs appeared to be made of a familiar rust-brown material, presumably the same high-dissipation polymer as the security cyborgs back home. The number of eye-like cameras scattered around the mid-line of their shell and the kind of joints connecting the phalanges of their mechanical hands, however, indicated that the unit in front of me was somewhat outmoded compared with the ones with which I was familiar. They were also larger than the ones used in my home-precinct.~~ Taking a step toward the cyborg, Major Azucena introduced me to Special Unit Deputy Bakola. ~~Their name and serial number appeared in stenciled, bulky white letters on their back and on the side of their left arm, the same left arm the Special Unit were extending toward me with an open hand. I was befuddled for a moment: the left hand? It took me a few~~

~~seconds to understand the situation. When I finally did, I reached for their mechanical appendage with my own left hand and shook it with a smile. It was significantly warmer than I anticipated.~~ Deputy Bakola stated gingerly that they were happy to make my acquaintance and looked forward to assisting me with this internal investigation.

SS8C-B1

Before entering the last room on the floor, B1, the chief knocked on the door. The room was roughly as large as the previous one but only had one small, inconveniently shaped window all the way in the far-right corner. The room hosted three workstations. An old man of South Asian descent occupied the rightmost of these—the one closest to the window. On his desk were a security terminal, a picture of a man and two children, and a copy of *Cond-Passion* magazine (the latest issue of the same periodical I had seen a few minutes earlier in the entrance hallway, B0). Special Unit Deputy Bakola followed us into the room, so I am drawing on their automatic transcript software to report the exchange that followed.

File ID: KC03
N.E. 330 – August 23, 11:17
[8C-SU Bakola (6584AR-4)]
(text automatically generated from video)

<Hestia Azucena ★★☆>: Uncle Rahman, good morning. I hope we're not interrupting.

<Rahman Kutta ★☆☆>: [Standing up] Hestia! To what do I owe the pleasure? Please come on in and make [inaudible].

<Hestia Azucena ★★☆>: [Walks toward Kutta] [Turns toward the door] Captain Tarkka, this is Captain Rahman Kutta, who we often refer to as "Uncle Rahman." [Speaking to Kutta] Uncle Rahman, it is with great pleasure that we are hosting Captain Elevii Agneta Tarkka, from all the way uptower.

<Rahman Kutta ★☆☆>: [Approaches] Delighted to make

your acquaintance, Captain.
[Extends his hand for a handshake].

<Elevii A. Tarkka ★☆☆>: Likewise, and happy to be here.
[Shakes Kutta's hand]

<Rahman Kutta ★☆☆>: What brings you to our sector, Capt—
[Appearing startled] Goodness! What is th—
[Takes a step back]
[Appearing agitated] Wh—what's that thing on your hand?

<Elevii A. Tarkka ★☆☆>: [Raises her right hand and looks at it] On my hand?

<Hestia Azucena ★★☆>: [Appearing distressed] *Diós*, this is so embarrassing!
[Turns to Tarkka] Captain, I am so, so sorry.

<Elevii A. Tarkka ★☆☆>: [Appears confused] [Inaudible]

At that point, Bakola tilted on their leg actuators. Their whirring can be heard distinctly in the recording.

<Hestia Azucena ★★☆>: We have barely even set foot in this office!
[Turns to Kutta]
[Appearing distressed] *Que demónios* is wrong with you?

<Rahman Kutta ★☆☆>: [Appearing agitated] What is wrong with me?! What's wrong with that thing!
[Pointing at Tarkka's hand]

<Self ☆>: [Speaking calmly] A modern LUNA model. And a two-thumber, too!
We are beyond jealous, Captain Tarkka.

<Hestia Azucena ★★☆>: [Interjecting] It's a cybernetic hand, old fool! Apologize to our guest!

<Elevii A. Tarkka ★☆☆>: [Appearing uncomfortable] I—it's okay, Major.

<Hestia Azucena ★★☆>: [Inaudible]

<Rahman Kutta ★☆☆>: It was... and [Inaudible] its extra finger, it... I—I am very sorry.

<Elevii A. Tarkka ★☆☆>: [Raises both hands in front of her] Really, don't worry about it. [Pauses] I understand LUNAs must not be common around these parts. And to be fair, I still get the occasional stare uptower, too.

<Rahman Kutta ★☆☆>: Again, please accept my apologies.
[Extends his hand again]

<Elevii A. Tarkka ★☆☆>: [Hesitates] [Shakes his hand]

<Rahman Kutta ★☆☆>: [Still holding Tarkka's hand] May I—
[Pauses] May I ask you what happened to it?

<Hestia Azucena ★★☆>: [Appearing exasperated] Okay, we're leaving now. I swear, It's...

<Elevii A. Tarkka ★☆☆>: [Interjecting] As I said, Major, it's okay. My accident is no secret, and Captain Kutta could even read a report about the whole thing in my security profile.

<Rahman Kutta ★☆☆>: Oh...

<Elevii A. Tarkka ★☆☆>: [Turns to Kutta] You see, my parents and I had just moved from midtower up to 78, so we were new to the area. One day, I was playing in a public area and happened to find a small gap in the insulating padding layers of the external wall. The aperture was barely large enough to fit my hand in, and that tiny version of me didn't know any better.
[Smiles] Long story short: stupid girl reaches in, and her sweaty hand sticks to the external layer of HOOS-MING ONE which, at that altitude, has a temperature close to sixty degrees below zero. My hand froze over almost instantly. It was, of course, very painful.
[Pauses] Eventually, they had to cut it off to set me free.
[Raises her cybernetic hand in front of her face] And, well... that was that.

[Repeatedly clenches and unclenches her mechanical fingers]

<Rahman Kutta ★☆☆>: Captain, allow me to repeat that I am terribly sorry for my reaction, and even sorrier about what happened to you.

<Elevii A. Tarkka ★☆☆>: Oh well... to be frank, it's been so long that I cannot even remember not having one of these.
[Tarkka's raised hand glows with colorful geometric patterns]

<Rahman Kutta ★☆☆>: [Appearing impressed] Look at that thing go!

<Hestia Azucena ★★☆>: [Speaking to Kutta] Thanks for that contribution, Captain Kutta. In case you're wondering what brings the young captain down from 78, Tarkka is here on a temporary transfer to lead an internal investigation.

<Rahman Kutta ★☆☆>: Oh...
[Pauses]
[Quietly] Of course. Kempinski.

My two-thumber stopped glowing at this point and went back to its usual inert matte-white color.

<Hestia Azucena ★★☆>: [Speaking to Kutta] And Room B2 is reserved for her investigation. Special Unit Deputy Bakola will be assisting Captain Tarkka.

<Rahman Kutta ★☆☆>: I had guessed as much.
[Turning to Us] An exciting new case, Deputy! Aren't you lucky now!

<Self ☆>: Indeed! We must admit that when the major told us... well, we had to pinch ourselves!
[We laugh]
Get it?! Pinching!

Uncle Rahman chortled in response to Bakola opening and closing their five-fingered hands as if they were pincers. Azucena shook her head, unamused.

<Hestia Azucena ★★☆>: Aside from making introductions, we are here because I imagined Captain Tarkka would appreciate having access to a more conventional workstation.

The major gestured toward the desk on the left, which was unused and ~~sadly~~ windowless.

<Hestia Azucena ★★☆>: You know, in case she prefers to have some company.
[Pauses] In retrospect, however...

<Elevii A. Tarkka ★☆☆>: Don't worry about that, Major, but I'm the kind of security officer who generally prefers to work alone. That's another thing about me that you could verify by checking my security profile. Please don't take this as me being ungrateful, but I feel it would be better if the Special Unit and I used the other room.

<Hestia Azucena ★★☆>: Well, Captain, whatever fills your sails. I guess it's settled, then.
[Pauses]
[Speaking to Tarkka] Keep in mind that, regardless of where you decide to work, Uncle Rahman's door will always be open to you. He can be a valuable source of information about the sector as well as our station.

<Rahman Kutta ★☆☆>: And I am always happy to lend a hand.

<NOTE> Unfortunate choice of words, there, for Uncle Rahman. The Special Unit trembled on their six legs, struggling to hold back a laugh. I guess this was when I realized the old captain was probably working alone here because of his interpersonal skills, or lack thereof. That is probably why he was conveniently isolated here, a long elevator ride away from the rest of the station's staff.
</NOTE>

<Hestia Azucena ★★☆>: [Speaking to Tarkka] Again, please don't hesitate to squeak if you need assistance.

<Elevii A. Tarkka ★☆☆>: [With a slight bow] Much appreciated.

<Hestia Azucena ★★☆>: [Nods] Right, off we go! [Leaves the room]

The automatically generated transcript did not report the awkward silence that followed the chief's departure. A moment later, Captain Kutta shook his head and sat back down at his desk, mumbling something about my case.

<Rahman Kutta ★☆☆>: [Inaudible]

<Elevii A. Tarkka ★☆☆>: Care to share what's on your mind?

<Rahman Kutta ★☆☆>: Oh, I just find it pretty unlucky that this tragic mess of a case was dumped on you so suddenly. And if you think about it, the fa— [Stops suddenly]
[Appearing tense] Wait. Is... is that normal?
[Pointing at Tarkka's hand] I mean, the thing your thing is doing now?

<Self ☆>: Oh boy.

<Elevii A. Tarkka ★☆☆>: [Squints] Do you mean my hand?

<Rahman Kutta ★☆☆>: I...

<Elevii A. Tarkka ★☆☆>: Captain, let me ask you a question instead. Is this a collegial, friendly conversation that we are having, here?

<Rahman Kutta ★☆☆>: Wh—what do you mean? I—

<Elevii A. Tarkka ★☆☆>: [Interrupting] From where I stand, it could look as if you are actively trying to provoke a reaction. Are you trying to find out how long it will take before the new kid loses her cool?

<Rahman Kutta ★☆☆>: Oh no! No, no... [Holding his hands up] The thing is— Well, your hand always seems to be... fidgeting. Whenever I look at it, it's doing... something!

<Elevii A. Tarkka ★☆☆>: Have you considered looking at it less?

I stared at him unflinchingly and then addressed Deputy Bakola without taking my eyes off Uncle Rahman.

<Elevii A. Tarkka ★☆☆>: Deputy, I believe we have burdened Captain Kutta with our presence for long enough. [Turns to leave]

<Self ☆>: [We begin to follow]

<Rahman Kutta ★☆☆>: [Appearing defensive] Yeah, w— well, I'm sorry! How am I supposed to know what's going on?! What if your thing was actually short-circuiting or something?

<Self ☆>: [We stop walking]
[We turn toward Kutta]
[Speaking calmly] Her hand is behaving normally, Captain. What you saw was not a malfunction or a seizure: it's called livenoting. Livenoting is a software extension for LUNA cybernetics that allows one to produce text extremely rapidly by means of micro-flexions of the phalanges. If it helps, you can think of it as a sort of technologically enhanced shorthand.

<NOTE> At this point in the recording, I took a deep breath. Then I exhaled, turned around, and walked back toward Captain Kutta. I raised my hand in front of him and livenoted this very sentence, making the text appear on the back of my LUNA for him to see. Maybe this would put an end to his questions and to our mutual embarrassment. For the first time since I had met him, Captain Kutta had nothing to say. </NOTE>

"Unbelievable. The guts of the motherfucker!" Inspector Pol Asciak whispers through gritted teeth.

This is the opening line of one of the two classified video extracts I received as part of the briefing package for my new case. The scene—file number two in our investigation repository—was recorded from the point of view of Special Unit Deputy Satia. Inspector Asciak and Deputy Satia are hiding in the entryway of an abandoned tenement at the center of Sector 8C. It is just before mid-day, but only a fraction of the natural light (itself not much more than an ashen twilight at that time of the year) reaches the interior areas of Column C through the combined use of skylights, shafts, and mirrors. Asciak is wearing civilian clothes, and is focusing on something happening across the street from the broken building where he and Satia are hiding.

From where they are crouching, the two officers have a direct line of sight to the dimly lit entrance of a small, run-down bar. The neon sign above the door says "Clem's." Lamentably, we cannot refer to points of view other than Satia's to verify how the following events unfolded. No public camera or garbage-removal automaton happened to be monitoring the street at that particular time. Granted, the area of Sector 8C where the video was shot is largely abandoned. It is, however, a tower-wide health and security directive that all commercial and administrative activities must keep continuous video recordings of the area in front of their entrances. This particular bar, however, did not comply with that requirement. At the time—and in an even more blatant defiance of safety regulations—there were also no security cameras capturing what happened *inside* Clem's bar.

It is precisely because of the scarcity of primary information sources that this internal investigation had to be launched. This case—my case—is the kind that video evidence would have automatically solved for us. Instead, though, we need to go through a lengthy process that relies on secondary sources and witness testimony. As mentioned earlier in this report, the events that followed were recorded through the exclusive and sadly incomplete perspective of Special Unit Deputy Satia.

File ID: KC02
N.E. 330 – August 14, 12.27
[8C-SU Satia (6584AR-5)]
(text automatically generated from video)

<Pol Asciak ☆☆☆>: Tell me I'm not fucking dreaming. Did they just walk into a bar?

<Self ☆>: We can confirm that the suspect has walked into an establishment called Clem's with Field Deputy Kempinski.

<Pol Asciak ☆☆☆>: What is he thinking?! The huge pile of bird shit...

<Self ☆>: We are unable to ascertain whether the suspect is carrying any weapons. He is just outside my scanners' range.

<Pol Asciak ☆☆☆> Tough luck, then. Looks like we're going to find out about that the old-fashioned way. [Takes a deep breath] Let's move!

In the video segment that follows, Investigator Asciak sprints away from the building from where he and Deputy Satia had been surveying the situation. The recording trails Asciak as he nimbly moves around abandoned vehicles and dashes across the street. ~~The inspector is broad shouldered and wears a long, dark coat. Deputy Satia, trotting on six pointy mechanical legs, follow him with remarkable smoothness.~~ Asciak reaches the door to Clem's bar and barges into the venue. Once inside, the Special Unit's camera eyes rapidly adapt to the brighter light. The bar's interior looks scuffed and dirty. Some ceiling panels are missing. ~~From these gaps, a gut-like mass of electrical wires and pipes herniates down into the room. Condensation drips from a ventilation duct onto one of the tables. It is hard to tell the color of the walls from Satia's video feed.~~ Tall, mismatched stools are lined up beside a narrow, zinc-topped bar that runs along one of the longer walls of the room. Behind the bar, a young-ish man with a thick moustache, scruffy eyebrows, and a dark apron is drying algae beer glasses. The cold interior lights make him look sickly. The interface overlay on the video feed identifies this man as Clem Young, the owner of the establishment. Opposite the bar's entrance, there are three doors, which presumably lead to storerooms or private drinking areas. A few alcoves line the wall across from the zinc-topped bar, but nobody is sitting there at the moment. Kitchen noises are coming from somewhere.

File ID: KC02
N.E. 330 – August 14, 12:29
[8C-SU Satia (6584AR-5)]
(text automatically generated from video)

<Pol Asciak ☆☆☆>: [Breathing heavily] [Speaking to Young] Where did he go?!

<Clem Young>: [Continuing to dry the glasses] Sorry, friend. We're still closed. Why don't you come back in an hour or so?

<Pol Asciak ☆☆☆>: [Appearing agitated] Where the fuck is he?

<Clem Young>: Hey, calm down.

<Pol Asciak ☆☆☆>: I will be calm once you tell me where Kempinski went. Talk!

At this point in the video, Young stops drying the glasses and slowly folds the towel he had been using. He puts this towel down beside the faucet and then calmly addresses Inspector Asciak.

<Clem Young>: Could you please be so kind as to introduce yourselves? I mean, this is—

<Pol Asciak ☆☆☆>: [Interrupting] —You damn well knew I was a security officer the second I walked into this shitty bar with a Special Unit. [Takes out his security identification badge]

<Clem Young>: [Appearing insecure] But how am I supposed to—
[Appearing apologetic] Look, I—

Pol Asciak grabs the bartender by his shirt, causing it to rip in a couple of places. Glasses rattle on the counter. A couple of them fall and shatter on the ground behind the bar. A dog, which never directly appears in the footage, yelps in surprise.

<Pol Asciak ☆☆☆>: [Through gritted teeth] I am going to ask you one more time, you bushy son of a bitch. [Speaking slowly] Where—

<Self ☆>: Inspector, why don't we...

<Pol Asciak ☆☆☆>: [Speaking slowly] the fuck— [Speaking slowly] did he go?

<Clem Young>: [Sighs]
[Nods toward one of the doors at the back of the bar]

<Pol Asciak ☆☆☆>: [Speaking to Satia] Deputy, you stay here and make sure nobody leaves this place. That includes our new best friend, here.

<Self ☆>: Acknowledged.

Inspector Asciak walks to the door that Clem Young indicated and disappears into the dark corridor behind it. In the main hall of the bar, Young does his best to make his torn shirt look presentable. The Special Unit's eyes follow Clem Young as he picks up a broom from a closet and begins to clean up the broken glass on the floor behind the bar. Nothing of note happens for a couple of minutes, and then Clem puts a kitchen towel across his right shoulder and addresses Deputy Satia.

<Clem Young>: Name's Clem. You know, like the bar.

<Satia ☆>: Deputy Satia, Station 8C. Pleasure to meet you, and sorry for the inconvenience. Does the dog have a name?

< Clem Young > The fleabag's called Hungry.

Here, the audio picks up the muffled sound of raised voices in a neighboring room.

<Self ☆>: Sorry about your shirt, Clem. And also about those glasses. Should you wish to claim for damages, we would be happy to provide the forms that will allow—

The muffled voices grow louder in the background of the Special Unit's footage. Then, there is a crash and a thud of some kind. And then silence. The bartender puts down the glass that he had been holding and turns his head toward the back of the bar. Nothing happens for a while. Clem shakes his head and mumbles something about how he would be calling security now if security officers were not already there. Deputy Satia appear to be unsure about what to do. After Clem's comment, the Special Unit take a few tentative steps toward the door through which their human colleague disappeared several minutes earlier but then stop in their tracks. The door, which Inspector Asciak left somewhat ajar, suddenly opens fully. Inspector Asciak is holding Field Deputy Kempinski, whose head is dangling lifelessly over the Inspector's right arm and bleeding profusely. In a state of shock, Asciak drags his unconscious colleague into the main hall of the bar.

"Call an emergency medical unit. Fuck," he says with a broken voice.

<NOTE> From Deputy Satia's interface overlay on the footage, we know that this request was superfluous, as the Special Unit automatically had already called for medical help milliseconds after they realized what they were looking at. </NOTE>

"It is on the way, Inspector. What's the status of the suspect?"

Asciak keeps dragging Kempinski, mumbling something unintelligible in response.

"Where is Vannevar?" press Deputy Satia. Then, without waiting for an answer, the Special Unit scuttle into the back room where the suspect, Egon Vannevar, is sitting still. He is in a private drinking booth, elbows on the table, hands clutching his balding head. Vannevar looks sickly and thin. He slowly turns his head and looks at Deputy Satia. The Special Unit scan the room and—after a quick assessment of the situation—start to recite the legal clauses and warnings that, following tower-wide procedures, precede an arrest. ~~As they list the rights of the suspect, the Special Unit's frontal cameras remain focused on the glistening, dark pool of blood that is expanding beneath the table.~~

INVESTIGATION DAY 2

August 24 – SS8C

~~When I arrived this morning, I found an old, slim paper book waiting for me on the table of Interview Room SS8C-B2. Sticking out from between its fibrous pages was a handwritten welcome note from Major Azucena.~~

~~A squeak search for the title of the book revealed that it was a relatively famous text written about three thousand years ago, an Old Era classic that readers praised for its tension between the characters' duties (burdens imposed on them by societal laws and customs) and individual sense of morality and justice. I wondered what to make of it.~~

With Deputy Bakola being off duty that day, I put my headgear on and started the day with some preparation work, beginning with re-watching both of the classified videos I had received as part of the briefing package.

The first of the two videos was recorded at a local diner in the night of July the 29th. It consisted of a lengthy and rather awkward conversation between Field Deputy Stanisław Kempinski and Inspector Pol Asciak after a work-related social event. I present the contents of this encounter in detail in a later section of this report.

The second piece of video evidence was the already-mentioned four-minute scene at Clem's bar, which was shot ten days ago.

~~The events captured in these two files marked, respectively, the beginning of a story and its tragic conclusion. My temporary transfer assignment in Sector 8 consisted of piecing together what happened to Field Deputy Kempinski behind that door in the back room of Clem's bar on the afternoon of August 14.~~

It might be relevant to mention that Deputy Bakola and I went through the latter video several times, adding notes and making sure not to miss any obvious clues. In a moment of rest between our repeated viewings, I informally asked Deputy Bakola about their level of acquaintance with Deputy Satia, the Special Unit who recorded this piece of video evidence. I did not mean to ask whether they had a close relationship; rather, I was seeking additional information that could be relevant in the interpretation of Satia's footage as well as in understanding their role in the Vannevar case, the investigation they had been working on when this event transpired. Deputy Bakola bluntly replied that they did not know much more about Deputy Satia than was publicly available in their security profile and the fact that they were both Special Units did not necessarily mean that they have a special bond, relationship, or knowledge about each other. "We don't hang out after work, if that's what you're asking," Bakola added.

<NOTE> It occurred to me that I have never thought about what Special Units do when they're not on duty. Do they have hobbies? Do they need sleep? And, in case they do, are their organic components still capable of dreaming? </NOTE>

The information on Moana Satia available in her security profile revealed that she used to be a Field Deputy on Luna. Satia was very young and new to the force when she died. She had been fatally wounded when her neck was deeply cut by a broken bottle during an uprising in Grimaldi City, a minor historical event that made the news in 322 as "The Clash of Grimaldi." That was over eight years ago. After the accident, according to the records, an enforcement vehicle rushed Satia to the closest hospital, but the ongoing riot had slowed vehicular traffic to a walking pace. As a result, Satia had lost too much blood during transit, and she stopped breathing just a few minutes before reaching the medical center. A bright side to this story, if we can agree to call it that, was that her brain and spinal cord had not been structurally damaged, so her wish to be reborn as a Special Unit could be fulfilled.

During our conversation, and with no additional prompting, Bakola mentioned that Satia's new body belonged to the same batch of Special Unit shells as their own. In a sense, Bakola added cheerfully, that makes them something like distant cousins. I smiled in response, and concluded that Moana Satia and Autumn Bakola must have died within a few weeks of one another.

~~A later check of Bakola's security profile confirmed that this was indeed the case: in fact, they had died just a few days apart. Deputy Bakola's case was as banal as it was unfortunate. She was off duty, enjoying a vacation with her wife after many years of non-stop service. They were traveling on a civil cruiser from LUNA to HOOS-MING ONE when a piece of cargo that had accidentally become dislodged crushed her ribcage. As a consequence of the trauma she suffered, Autumn Bakola died a week later in a HOOS-MING ONE hospital in Sector 80, near the top of the megatower. That was just a couple of days before "The Clash of Grimaldi." I also ran a query on Autumn Bakola's widow. Apparently, still lives on LUNA, works as a teacher, has remarried, and is consistently late in submitting her income declaration forms.~~

I am reporting this interaction with the Special Unit assisting on my internal investigation because, earlier that morning, I happened to encounter Deputy Satia. I was on the main floor of the security station on my way down to B2 when I saw them walking in a corridor. ~~We had never met in person before, but Deputy Satia were easy to identify because of their name and registration number stenciled over their shell. I caught up with them and introduced myself. Deputy Satia indeed inhabited the same, slightly outdated model as Bakola.~~ Satia scanned my face and badge and promptly understood both who I was and the reason for my presence there. They were friendly and eager to inform me that the entirety of their recordings for the Vannevar case—the recordings on which most of my own investigation was going to rely—had been uploaded and encrypted in the station's digital archives and should be accessible in full at my clearance level. I thanked them and followed with what I unfortunately framed as a personal question: I asked Deputy Satia how they were feeling about what happened to Kempinski. In response, they stated that they would be more than happy to talk about their perspectives in the context of a formal deposition, should the investigation get to that point. With a candor that is not uncommon among Special Units, they added that their personal feelings were irrelevant to my investigation—or should be anyway. I admitted that both were fair points.

For context, the security protocol for internal investigations is clear on how this kind of work should be performed: in the interest of limiting the spread of information and to avoid the cross-contamination of depositions, I was to begin by collecting formal statements from the human staff members who were directly tied to the case. With their comment about the investigation potentially "getting to that point," Deputy Satia were specifically referring to the fact that they would only be asked for an official deposition in the improbable event that my case could not be closed on the basis of factual proof and human testimony. To be sure, Deputy Satia could always volunteer to put their side of the story—that is, their account of the investigative work concerning the Vannevar case—on the record, but the ability to directly provide all relevant footage made the need for a deposition extremely unlikely.

~~With Field Deputy Kempinski out of the picture, my first step had to be obtaining a complete deposition from Inspector Pol Asciak. Simply put, from the start, there was not much room for maneuver concerning how to lead my investigation. As it turned out, I would not be able to decide how or when to end it, either.~~

Later on the same day, I squeak-called the station's legal office and asked them to issue an order to appear for Inspector Asciak for the following morning (August 25). ~~It would have been impractical, and indelicate, to ask Deputy Bakola to take care of this part of the process on their day off. As an unnecessary courtesy, I sent them a message to inform them about the new agenda item that I added to our shared calendar.~~

<NOTE> Here, I characterize my action as "unnecessary" because Bakola would be automatically notified of any additions or other

changes to our case calendar or repository. </NOTE>

Given Inspector Asciak's direct involvement in this investigation, he was suspended from work and temporarily banned from station grounds. His access to security files and his permission to leave the megatower—or even to travel between the sectors of this column—was revoked for the time being. ~~From the little I knew about him, Pol Asciak did not seem like someone who would be particularly fond of waiting or who would enjoy sitting at home for days on end. My guess is that he had been impatiently waiting for his order to appear for a couple of days at this point.~~ In preparation for Asciak's upcoming deposition, I spent the rest of the day gathering background information and revisiting the security records of the few people currently listed as persons of interest in my case. The list obviously included both Pol Asciak and Stanisław Kempinski. I also examined the security database for information concerning Egon Vannevar—the lanky, balding, distraught man who was arrested by Deputy Satia in Clem Young's bar. Finally, I looked up the records for Clement Young himself. Below is a quick breakdown of the relevant information I collected:

<u>Inspector Pol Asciak (Male, 39, Sector 8C – HOOS-MING ONE)</u>: First in his class and captain of the wrestling team at the security academy, Asciak appears to have been a well-liked member of Security Station 8C ever since he joined the force. That was sixteen years ago. As far back as his performance reviews go, Asciak has been unfailingly praised, with adjectives such as "reliable," "thorough," and "supportive" coming up repeatedly. Exceptionally efficient with his cases and without a single disciplinary note tarnishing his record of accomplishments, Asciak is presented as a paragon of virtue: the cream of the crop. Additional profile details mark him as right-handed, single, and mildly allergic to mushroom flour. He is listed both as an organ donor and a candidate to be reborn as a Special Unit. By the looks of it, it will not be long until his promotion to the rank of captain.

<u>Field Deputy Stanisław "Stan" Kempinski (Male, 64, Byrgius – Moon)</u>: Kempinski was born on Luna and had served on the security forces there for most of his career. He obtained a transfer to HOOS-MING ONE a little over six years ago, following a separation from his wife (Dr. Grace Kempinski, née Grace Tizzi).

Judging by results alone, Kempinski is one of the most successful officers at Station 8C. His professional attainments are not, however, accompanied by the profile of a disciplined, hardworking officer. His performance reviews often mention him being lazy, stubborn, and uncooperative. His disregard for authority is glaringly clear in the dozens of disciplinary notes and warnings attached to his profile. Kempinski's infractions range from showing up late for work (or not showing up at all) to using investigative methods that could be described as "unconventional." Kempinski's professional toolkit apparently includes lies, threats, and bribes. He is also known to occasionally drink on duty. I spotted a couple of notes on his personal hygiene, too. Field Deputy Kempinski is left-handed, and he is listed as neither an organ donor nor a volunteer for the Special Unit rebirth program. This means that, even if the relevant parts of his brain and nervous system had somehow miraculously escaped damage from what happened in the back room of Clem's bar, Kempinski would not return as a Special Unit. In the six years he has worked at Station 8C, he never partnered with Inspector Asciak until the most recent case. This changed with the Vannevar case for reasons that will become apparent in the following sections of this report.

Egon Vannevar (Male, 62, Grimaldi City – Moon): ~~On the topic of the Vannevar case, here is what I could find about the main suspect himself.~~ Egon Vannevar's identity records are skeletal, consisting solely of a name, origin, and a couple of trivial security entries. Vannevar apparently has no partners or divorces, no children or relatives, and no major security infractions. Two troubling aspects of his profile are the lack of facial scans and the fact that his records do not list his recent arrest. Concerned with these blatant irregularities, I went on the squeak networks using my terminal to look for additional information about Egon Vannevar, but the name did not show up in any news networks or databases. Determined to get to the bottom of this, I called the sector's mainframe. ~~An artificial clerk answered my call and, following detailed legal protocols, introduced themselves as a T2 artificial intelligence. Would I like to continue anyway, it asked? I scanned my badge, vocalized my consent, and was granted access to the database. I only had one question for the artificial clerk: did my credentials grant me complete access to the security profile of Egon Vannevar? Was what I was examining his full profile?~~

The voice on the other end of the call confirmed that I did have complete access and that no parts of this record were censored or classified at a level of clearance higher than the one currently associated with my profile. The clerk also commented that, statistically speaking, the level of information contained in this particular profile was highly irregular. I asked when the profile was created and received an answer that added to my concerns, as it dated back only a little over two months.

In the afternoon, troubled by what I had just found, I sent a lengthy squeak-message to Major Azucena. In it, I gave a detailed account of the abnormalities I noted in Vannevar's profile and commented on the recency of its creation. Vannevar's file would be able to pass only a cursory screening, which was a likely indication of a ~~fairly clumsy~~ security breach. I advised the chief to look into the situation with the utmost priority.

<NOTE> I felt, of course, that these glaring irregularities should have been spotted weeks before and should have prompted Azucena to take urgent action then. Even that early in my investigation, I thought it unconscionable that Kempinski had been so sloppy that he failed notice something like that. </NOTE>

<u>Clement "Clem" Young (Male, 37, Sector 8C – HOOS-MING ONE)</u>: Finally, Clement Young. The owner of the small, run-down bar in the dead center of Sector 8, Column C. Because of the events that took place on his business premises, Young—as a potential witness—is also not allowed to leave the sector. Although the forensic team has already concluded their ~~rather inconclusive~~ report, Young is also not to be allowed to reopen his bar until a security camera system feeding directly into the sector's mainframe is installed in the establishment, in compliance with tower-wide regulations. The building is co-owned by Young and his mother~~, but this is not strictly relevant~~. A number of infractions are listed under Young's name in the security database, the most severe of which relates to him having illegally produced and dealt a cheap kind of homemade drug. Four years ago, he was arrested and incarcerated because of that. I am familiar with the drug in question, whose highly addictive active principle is synthesized from the same ammonia used as a refrigerant in the thermo-syphons of megatowers. Young was eventually released on bail

posted by his mother and has apparently been on the straight and narrow ever since. A curious detail: the lead officer on the case that led to the arrest of Clement Young was ~~none other than~~ Field Deputy Kempinski.

INVESTIGATION DAY 3

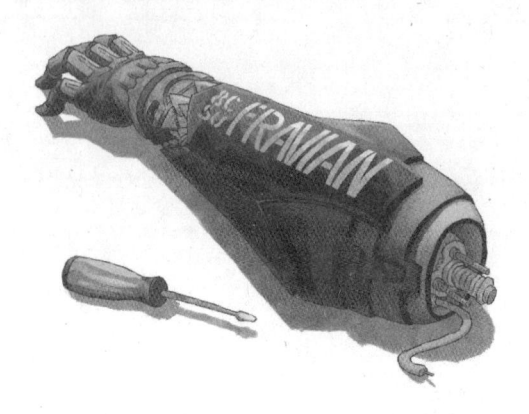

August 25 – SS8C

The following morning, Pol Asciak arrived at the station before I did. When I reached Floor B, he was already sitting on the bench in the waiting area outside the elevator. ~~Asciak was wearing a suit, and his light-brown hair was scrupulously parted on the right side.~~

<NOTE> I remember thinking that he seemed to have lost a substantial amount of weight compared with the profile pictures and video footage I had seen up to that point. </NOTE>

~~Judging by his posture, Asciak must have been waiting there for quite a while already, although it was still a half hour before the time scheduled for the first deposition session to begin. When he saw me exit the elevator, he stood up, put the magazine he was reading back on the small table between the two bench seats, and approached me for a handshake. The absence of a surprised reaction when he touched my cybernetic hand probably meant he had looked up information on who was going to be responsible for this internal investigation (and, perhaps, for the trajectory the rest~~

~~of his career).~~ To break the ice, I nodded toward the magazine he had been reading and asked him whether he was into the popular card game to which the publication was dedicated. Asciak replied that he had not cared much about *Duplicate Conduit* before the Vannevar case. There are many fascinating aspects to the game, he explained, including its serendipitous discovery and the quirks of its professional competitive scene. Knowing close to nothing about *Duplicate Conduit*, I quickly livenoted a reminder to myself to look up these aspects of the game later.

A longhaired woman was collecting some snacks from the vending machine on the other side of the room. I only became aware of her presence when the nutrient bars clunked against the bottom of the machine. Pol Asciak introduced the woman as Merel Asciak, his sister. With casual ease, Merel added that she was also Pol's lawyer and that, as was his federal right, she would be providing legal assistance to her brother during the deposition. "Legal assistance that I do not need, by the way," was Pol Asciak's response to his sister's words. Then, he followed with what could only be qualified as an open admission of guilt: "Your investigation is in fact very easy, Captain. I did it. I killed Kempinski."

<NOTE> In retrospect, I think one of the hardest parts of coming to terms with what was happening was reconciling Asciak's outstanding security profile with the behavior of the individual standing in front of me. </NOTE>

Merel Asciak joined us by the bench and took a long, silent look at her brother. Clearly less dazed than I was, she then quietly turned to me and asked whether the spontaneous outburst of her "shit-for-brains brother" could be kept off the record. Merel tried to give context to her brother's confession: Pol was not a murderer, she explained, and what he meant to say was that he had played a significant role in the sequence of events that had ultimately led to Field Deputy Kempinski's tragic accident. ~~I said nothing, still overwhelmed by what was happening. Then my right hand lit up and buzzed with a reminder I had set for myself: thirty minutes to go until the start of the first session. The abrupt perceptual stimulation jolted me back to the "here and now" and helped me to regain focus.~~ I informed Pol and Merel Asciak that Kempinski had not died yet, although his condition remained critical. I also let them know that the room we were in was not monitored by cameras, meaning that there would be no objective "record" of what had just happened, but that I would still have to include the contents of our interaction in my report. Merel nodded. Of course, she said, adding with a reassuring tone that her brother would soon clarify the extent of his responsibility in the unfortunate events under investigation.

Moments later, I scanned my badge and entered the interview room alone. There, I found Deputy Bakola already crouched on top of one of the chairs surrounding the table, facing the door. ~~They, too, must have been there for a while: briefing notes and postplastic drinking glasses had been distributed around the table, and the water pitcher had been filled.~~

I noticed that a dozen small, crustacean-looking automata were moving around on the external surface of the room's enormous window, ~~cleaning the glass panels in a coordinated fashion that was oddly dance-like. Flat finger-like extremities at the end of their mechanical legs allowed them to negotiate the strong winds and the smoothness of the surfaces on which they were moving in a way that looked effortless.~~ Concerned about the confidentiality hazard posed by the cameras on the automata outside the window, I asked Bakola whether they had a way to communicate with the sector mainframe or with the service automata themselves and postpone their operations. The Special Unit replied, jokingly, that they could use their enforcement capabilities to disable the little droids, but that would be a waste of perfectly good T1 intelligences. Instead, Deputy Bakola buzzed a command to the room's control system, which caused the view of the central syphon and the other columns of the megatower to fade from view, leaving a shadowy blankness of indeterminate depth. The curved, dark wall also functions as a terminal screen, the Special Unit informed me. ~~As the glass wall turned into a completely opaque surface, the homeostatic lighting system shifted to compensate for the decrease in luminosity in the room by emitting a diffuse, artificial radiance.~~

Pol and Merel Asciak knocked on the metal door of Room B2 at the appointed time. After introducing themselves to Deputy Bakola, the siblings took their seats next to one another. The Special Unit climbed down from the chair where they were crouched and moved to another one in front of the Asciaks, ready to record their account in this morning's session. The following section of this report was extracted from Bakola's footage.

File ID: KC03
N.E. 330 – August 25, 09:58
[8C-SU Bakola (6584AR-4)]
(text automatically generated from video)

<Elevii A. Tarkka ★☆☆>: So, this is the beginning of the deposition of Inspector Pol Asciak in the context of—

<Pol Asciak>: [Interrupting] "Mister."

<Elevii A. Tarkka ★☆☆>: [Turning toward Pol Asciak] Excuse me?

<Pol Asciak>: I was released from my security duties. It's Mister Asciak now.

<Elevii A. Tarkka ★☆☆>: [Turns toward Merel Asciak]

<Merel Asciak>: [Shrugs]

<Elevii A. Tarkka ★☆☆>: [Turns back to Pol Asciak] Of course. You are technically right, even though my briefing information states that your suspension is only meant as a temporary measure.
[Takes a deep breath] Well, then, correcting my previous statement, this is the beginning of the deposition of *Mister* Pol Asciak regarding his involvement in the Vannevar case. His testimony is part of the evidentiary body of the internal investigation that I am conducting. It is the 25th of August, 330.
[Checks the back of her right hand] The time is 10 o'clock in the morning. Pol Asciak is assisted in this deposition by his legal representative, Miss Merel Asciak, who is attending in person.
[Turns to Merel Asciak] Miss Asciak, allow me to remind you that, in your advisory role, you can request breaks and private consultations with your client, but you must not contribute to the deposition. Is this understood?

<Merel Asciak>: Yes, Captain. Thank you.
[Takes a sip of water from the glass in front of her]

<Elevii A. Tarkka ★☆☆>: [Turns back to Pol Asciak] Mister Asciak, as I mentioned in my opening statement, this hearing has the objective of gathering information about the Vannevar case, which you were a part of together with Field Deputy Kempinski.

<Pol Asciak>: [Interjecting] And Deputy Satia, yes.

<Elevii A. Tarkka ★☆☆>: Of course. This is also an opportunity for you to officially state your perspective on the events that took place in the last three weeks. If you agree, and for the sake of clarity, I would like you to share your side of the story, starting from the very beginning—that is, when you heard of Egon Vannevar for the first time.

<Pol Asciak>: [Pauses] I... hmm, I assume you're talking about the station party at New Era?

<Elevii A. Tarkka ★☆☆>: Indeed. That social event was identified by the automated software that analyzes security footage as the beginning of your involvement in the case, or at least the first time Vannevar's name appears in footage where you are present. This is the information I was given. Should the 29th of June be inaccurate as the start of your involvement, or if you had previously discussed details concerning the case with Field Deputy Kempinski, please feel free to set the record straight.

<Pol Asciak>: [Shakes his head] No... yeah, I think the night of the party would be the place to start.

<Elevii A. Tarkka ★☆☆>: We have a recording of that conversation. My personal preference would be to watch the scene at the New Era Diner together on that screen. [Gestures toward the currently opaque glass] We can pause the video at any time so that you can add contextual information or personal comments whenever needed. In my experience, that makes it less likely for us to overlook any details that might be important for the investigation. Would that be all right?

<Pol Asciak>: [Nods] Sure.

I asked Deputy Bakola to enable the screen controls to allow me to pair the wall of glass in front of us with my terminal. Moments later, using my LUNA, I opened a menu and played the video that I had prepared for this deposition session. ~~Following my command, the automated light system in the interrogation room automatically reduced the intensity of the ambient illumination.~~

The video extract was taken from continuous security camera footage monitoring the interior of a Sector 8 dining establishment called New Era. The time on the video's interface overlay indicates that it is almost twelve in the night of July the 29th. The party is almost over. ~~Festive decorations droop from the walls of the diner, and the security staff members who are still hanging around are talking in small groups, their glasses mostly empty.~~ A few seconds into the video segment I had extracted, the background music is switched off, which significantly improves the intelligibility of the audio and makes the use of facial topology-aided speech recognition unnecessary.

In the foreground of one of the points of view of the security cameras inside the diner, Field Deputy Stanisław Kempinski is sitting alone at the bar, not far from the main entry/exit door of the diner. He is clearly overweight and practically bald, save for the white stubble on the sides of his head. Kempinski looks significantly older than the age stated in his personal profile. His light-yellow shirt is a collection of wrinkles and both new and old food stains. A folded piece of white paper sticks clumsily out of his patch pocket. In front of Kempinski is a large beer glass that only appears to contain foam residue. Half a minute into the recording, a woman walks behind Kempinski, making her way toward the exit. "Good night, old boy!" she says, patting Kempinski on the back, her speech slurred. Kempinski smiles and salutes his colleague. He then gulps down the last few drops of whatever was left in his glass.

Moments later, a four-armed, black-aproned android approaches Kempinski from across the bar. "I see that your glass is empty, sir. Would you like another one?"

Kempinski shrugs and answers, "And what would I do with two empty glasses?"

The artificial intelligence pauses, as if to collect its thoughts:

"There must have been a misunderstanding, sir. Let me rephrase my question. We will soon close the bar; is it your intention to place a last order?"

Kempinski smiles and asks for two pints of algae beer.

The large windows of the diner face inward onto a snug public hub surrounded by a handful of other bars and restaurants. Except for one, all the other establishments in this small cluster have already closed up shop for the night. Inside the New Era Diner and Café, a security staff member heads toward the door, and another one follows soon after. The automated software interface identifies the second person as Inspector Pol Asciak of Station 8C.

Kempinski, who has remained for the most part indifferent to everything happening around him until this point, shows a newly awakened interest when he sees Asciak heading discretely toward the door.

"Well, if it isn't the party boy!" Kempinski hails him, almost shouting.

Asciak stops in his tracks and turns toward the stubbly man at the bar. His body language indicates without a doubt that he does not want to spend an additional minute in this place, or with this man.

"Welcome back and congratulations on another closed case, Inspector!"

Kempinski spins on his barstool and extends a hand to Asciak to make his congratulations physical as well.

"Much appreciated, man, thank you," replies Asciak, who then takes a couple of steps toward the field deputy and shakes his hand.

"And the trick with the little service crab. Boy, that was great stuff. Creative, too!"

<NOTE> They shook hands for longer than I would consider friendly or polite. Asciak smiled awkwardly, which I guess was due to the combination of the prolonged physical contact and Kempinski's oddly specific interest in Asciak's latest investigation. </NOTE>

"Yeah, the service automaton. We do try our best, right? Look, Kempinski, I need to go get some sleep. I barely made it back in time for the party and am scheduled to be on duty tomorrow morning."

"No rest for the wicked, huh? Come on, I'm sure you have time for one last drink."

"I... I really shouldn't."

Kempinski takes one of the two freshly poured algae beers he previously ordered and hands it to Asciak. The inspector sighs, takes the glass, and sits on a barstool next to his colleague.

> <Pol Asciak>: Captain, could we please pause for a second here?
>
> <Elevii A. Tarkka ★☆☆>: [Pauses the video] Of course we can.
>
> <Pol Asciak>: I... I just wanted to clarify that Kempinski and I were not close. We had never worked together before, let alone hung out socially.
> This part of the video might... might give the wrong impression.
>
> <Elevii A. Tarkka ★☆☆>: I wanted to ask about that. The two of you had never worked together before the Vannevar case, which struck me as quite odd. You know, with this being a relatively small station and all.
>
> <Pol Asciak>: I had expressed a preference not to work with Kempinski... not as a formal request, to be clear. It's just something I asked the boss. Informally, that is. [Pauses] Some... some people don't mind Kempinski's— let's call it "style," but...
> [Shrugs]
>
> <Elevii A. Tarkka ★☆☆>: [Interrupting] But that's not the case with you—is that what you're saying?
>
> <Merel Asciak>: [Clears her throat emphatically]
>
> <Pol Asciak>: [Speaking to Tarkka] Look, Kempinski has a reputation for being hard to work with. His results

notwithstanding, most officers at our station consider him an undesirable partner.

<Elevii A. Tarkka ★☆☆>: You present this as a matter of character and a commonly shared opinion. Where do you *personally* stand in relation to those ideas?

<Pol Asciak>: At the time, I remember thinking that I could never work with someone as self-centered and erratic as he is.

<Elevii A. Tarkka ★☆☆>: And yet you did.

<Pol Asciak>: That was not my call, Captain.

<Elevii A. Tarkka ★☆☆>: Yes, and we will come back to that point. For now, let's go back to what we just watched.

<Pol Asciak>: [Shrugs] Okay.

<Elevii A. Tarkka ★☆☆>: You looked uncomfortable with shaking Kempinski's hand and even with sitting next to him.

<Pol Asciak>: Yeah. I was not thrilled to be there. I suppose that much is evident. I was tired and had no desire to deal with his sudden interest in my work.

<Elevii A. Tarkka ★☆☆>: I see. [Pauses, appearing to think] Just one last thing about the footage we just watched—and this is mostly out of personal curiosity: Kempinski mentioned a... [Checks the notes on the palm of her artificial hand] a "trick with the little service crab." What was that about?

<Pol Asciak>: [Gestures toward the screen] This station party was one of two that the station hosts every year, usually at that very diner. In this particular case, the event also coincided with my return from Sector 79, where I testified in the trial of two corrupt security officers working in customs at the spaceport. You may have heard about the case.

<Elevii A. Tarkka ★☆☆>: I did hear about it, of course. It was all over the news networks! You led a spectacularly successful inter-sector investigation. Smuggling and corruption, was it?

<Pol Asciak>: Black market tech and ammonia, yeah. The occasional weapon, too.

<Elevii A. Tarkka ★☆☆>: Outstanding work—well worth celebrating, if you ask me.

<Pol Asciak>: Well, thank you. [Scratches his cheek] Anyway, the service automaton trick that Kempinski was referring to is something I came up with toward the end of that investigation. We were after a small criminal organization operating out of a warehouse here in 8C, pretty much at the center of the column.

Bakola's leg actuators whirred audibly as they adjusted their position on the chair.

<Pol Asciak>: When we finally closed in on our suspects, we made an unconventional strategic decision. Instead of storming into the warehouse hoping to find enough contraband, we opted to reprogram a service automaton. I'm talking about one of those little T1 droids that pick up the trash, repair pipes, clean windows, stuff like that.

<Elevii A. Tarkka ★☆☆>: I know the kind. Please continue.

<Pol Asciak>: Well, our plan was to use it to infiltrate the space where they were running their smuggling operations by going through their ventilation system. And for that, the little automaton had to come in from the outside and travel all the way from the air filters on the surface of the column to one of Choksi's aeration grids.

<NOTE> Here, Asciak is referring to Hematsu "Hemu" Choksi, the centerpiece of the investigation being discussed. At the time of Asciak's deposition, Choksi was still awaiting his trial in the detention center shared by Sectors 8 and 9. </NOTE>

<Pol Asciak>: From there, our automaton filmed the inside of the warehouse for three straight days. And that's how we got our incriminating evidence regarding both Choksi and the two dirty security officers involved in the operation.

<Elevii A. Tarkka ★☆☆>: Thank you for your explanation.

> Everything is clear now. Unless you want to provide additional comments or supplementary information, I suggest that we resume the video.
>
> <Pol Asciak>: Please.
> [Takes a sip from the glass of water in front of him]

I resumed playing the extract with Kempinski and Asciak sitting and drinking at the bar. For the first two or three minutes of their interaction, they try to overcome their shared unease with a few stunted attempts at small talk. In the frequent pauses in their exchange, the world of New Era chatters and clinks away in the background. At one point, Kempinski praises Asciak for his physical condition, to which the investigator responds by sarcastically asking, "When did *you* last hit the gym?"

"The gym?! I do get plenty of exercise at work: I dodge meetings, push my luck, and jump to conclusions multiple times a day!"

Asciak chortles and comments that it would be nice if Kempinski also bothered to shower, after all that.

~~In the interrogation room, Merel Asciak barely manages to choke back a laugh.~~

In the video on the wall-sized screen, Kempinski laughs at Asciak's remark. "Good one, Inspector," he says, patting his younger colleague on his back, "but that's enough fucking around now."

"Oh, you mean you're finally going to tell me why I'm sitting here? You've never bought me a drink before or even tried to hit on me. As I said before, it's late and I'm tired, so why don't you cut to the chase—what is it that you want from me?"

Kempinski shrugs. "I don't want anything from you, bub," he says innocently.

Asciak smiles and shakes his head in evident disbelief. Then he takes a sip of his algae beer.

"What I had in mind was quite the opposite, in fact," continues Kempinski. "I'd like to do something for you!"

"Oh, would you now?!" replies Asciak, turning toward Kempinski in a comically exaggerated display of attention.

"I would like to offer you some help with the Choksi case."

"The Choksi case?" Asciak lets out a loud, nervous laugh. "This party is partly in celebration of the successful closing of that investigation, old man. Choksi and his goons will face trial, and there's enough evidence to keep them in the slammer until the ice comes back. Now, if you'll excuse me—"

"Fine, fine..." Kempinski concedes, "it's not exactly the Choksi case. But it's close enough. You see, I'm talking about a... let's call it a continuation of that investigation."

"I think you've had too much to drink tonight." Asciak stands up to leave, abandoning his half-full glass of beer on the bar.

Kempinski puts a hand on Asciak's arm, stopping him in his tracks. "Here's the thing, Pol. May I call you Pol? Whatever. Look, I had the opportunity to examine the footage your droid captured in Choksi's hideout, and—"

"—Hrm?!"

"As it turns out, your little crab fortuitously captured something odd. Something... troubling. I'm talking about stuff that's potentially bigger than a few barrels of smuggled ammonia."

Asciak is visibly annoyed at the dismissive tone Kempinski is using to describe his recent success. "Get to the point. What's this about? Just tell me."

"I'm going to do more than tell you. I'm going to show you!"

Kempinski takes a gulp of his dark green drink. Nothing else happens in the footage for a while, adding to the awkward and unrhythmic quality of the conversation. Asciak looks at Kempinski, who, seemingly unaware, stares in contemplation at the liqueur bottles across the bar.

"So?!"

"Huh?"

"Weren't you going to show me something? Some unsettling material related to my investigation?"

"I— I said I was going to, bub, but I didn't mean right now. First,

I don't have my terminal with me, and second, it's nearly drunk o'clock. Far too late to talk serious shop, don't you agree? Would you... hmm... How about tomorrow in my office?"

Once again, Asciak shakes his head bitterly. What did I do to deserve this, his body language screams. Kempinski wipes light green beer foam from his mouth with the back of his hand. "Look, can I speak candidly, Inspector?"

"That's what I've been wondering for the past ten minutes. *Can* you?!"

"I wanted to have this conversation with you tonight because it's the decent thing to do, and much preferable to you finding out on your own tomorrow."

"Finding out what, exactly?"

"Well, that you and I are working this new case together."

Silence.

"After all," Kempinski continues after a brief pause, "it is an offshoot of your old case that we're talking about, and with your experience... I mean, it's a no-brainer that you need to be on the team!"

<Elevii A. Tarkka ★☆☆>: [Pauses the video]

[Speaking to Pol Asciak] Any comments?

<Pol Asciak>: [Shakes his head]

<Elevii A. Tarkka ★☆☆>: There's not much recorded material left in this particular video. Is it okay to continue?

<Pol Asciak>: Sure.

The on-screen version of Asciak sits back down on the barstool and stares at the glass of algae beer in front of him.

"I don't like you, Kempinski. Never have."

"Yeah, I picked up on that from a few clues, here and there."

Asciak turns toward Kempinski and asks, "Then why? I mean, why not work this case with a Special Unit instead? Our station has three you can choose from!"

"I hate to be the bearer of more bad news, but we have only two crabs left. While you were up at 79 for the deposition, Deputy Fravian died."

Asciak must have been thinking his evening couldn't get any worse at that point.

"I was only away for four days..."

"Yup. A malfunction with the cooling system during a routine patrol at the center of the column, at night. They couldn't find help in time, and the poor thing practically boiled alive inside their shell. What a way to go, huh?"

Kempinski raises his glass, presumably as a way to honor their departed colleague.

"Fuck..." mutters Asciak. They both remain silent for half a minute or so.

Once again, it is Kempinski who breaks the silence. "To answer your question," he says, "I'd rather work with humans any day of the week. Still speaking candidly, I don't think crabs make good pigs."

Asciak readjusts his posture on the barstool, presumably as a reaction to his older colleague's casual use of slur to refer to Special Units.

"Take dum-dum, over there." Kempinski gestures toward the android who is standing behind the bar, not far from where the two security officers are sitting. "It can make cocktails, serve beers, clean up, automatically send orders to suppliers, and even pretend to care about the lives of regular customers. The lights are all on, but nobody's home, if you catch my drift."

"Hmm."

"No offense intended, buddy," Kempinski says to the android.

"None taken, sir."

"My point exactly!" Kempinski exclaims after turning back to Asciak.

"Seriously, now. You can't be comparing a T2 android with a Special Unit. Come on!"

"I guess that's what I just did. And please spare me the whole 'crabs are not mere machines' spiel—that a significant part of them is biologically alive and all that. As far as I'm concerned, when everything they say or do is filtered through a mechanical ghost that haunts their shell, it's a machine that I'm talking to."

"That ghost being the T3 intelligence keeping them alive?"

"You call *that* living?!" Kempinski is getting fired up. "Me, I'd rather be dead than dancing to someone else's music. Also, they have a shit sense of humor and cannot take a single, tiny step beyond the boundaries of the law. Not even a teeny-weeny infraction in service of the greater good! Can you imagine ever getting any security work done like that?"

"As I see it, the fact that they cannot bully suspects, cut deals with criminals, or lie under oath makes Special Units better and more reliable security officers than humans, not worse. And on the theme of breaking the law, maybe you would care to explain how you managed to get your hands on still-undisclosed material from my investigation!"

"Let's not get side-tracked with details, Inspector. The point here is that I would rather work with you than with any crab."

"I wouldn't be surprised if the Special Units felt the same way about you."

<NOTE> I remember observing Deputy Bakola, curious as to their reaction to the conversation. The Special Unit, however, did not show any detectable response. </NOTE>

The progress gauge at the bottom of the video showed that there was not much footage left in this particular recording. In the video, Asciak stands up and says, "So I guess I will meet you tomorrow morning."

"Fat chance, bub. I'm going to marinate my sorrows in a few more drinks and take the morning off. Call in sick, whatever. How about the afternoon?"

Asciak mumbles something inaudible and walks out of the diner at last. In the background, the main hall of New Era is now empty, and its lights have been turned off. Kempinski is alone at the bar, the last customer in the whole diner. In the last few seconds of the video, he is trying to convince the bartender-android to serve him another drink.

<Merel Asciak>: [Yawns with a hand over her mouth]

<Elevii A. Tarkka ★☆☆>: [Speaking to Pol Asciak] All right, is there anything you want to add before we move on?

<Pol Asciak>: Nothing that I can think of.

<Elevii A. Tarkka ★☆☆>: Would you be so kind as to tell me what happened after that?

<Pol Asciak>: I... Well, I went home. I think I squeak-called my girlfriend and then went to bed straight after that. The following morning, on my way to my appointment with Azucena, I passed by Kempinski's office, but the door was closed. No surprises there, nor in the meeting that followed. The chief simply confirmed what Kempinski had told me the night before. Stan and I would form the unlikely investigative team tasked with working a spin-off from my previous case.

<Elevii A. Tarkka ★☆☆>: Going back to something you said: your partner—your girlfriend—she doesn't live with you, right?

<Pol Asciak>: She does not. As a matter of fact, she doesn't even live in this sector. Vicky is from 79B. I... we met a little over three weeks ago.

<Elevii A. Tarkka ★☆☆>: When you were transferred uptower, I see...

<Merel Asciak>: [Raising a hand] I'm sorry to interrupt, Captain, but I fail to see how my client's personal life is relevant to this deposition.

<Elevii A. Tarkka ★☆☆>: [Speaking to Merel Asciak] The information might not be presently useful or relevant but has the potential to become such. Think, for example, about the need to corroborate an alibi, or to cross-validate information relevant to the case. Mind you, I'm not saying your client needs an alibi. All I'm trying to convey here is that gathering that kind of information is well within the remit of my mandate.

<Merel Asciak>: Hmm...

<Elevii A. Tarkka ★☆☆>: [Speaking to Pol Asciak] What is her full name?

<Pol Asciak>: Victoria Lee. Field Deputy Victoria Lee.

<ELEVII'S LUNA> Deputy Bakola, please retrieve Field Deputy Victoria Lee's security profile and add it to our repository.

<Elevii A. Tarkka ★☆☆>: During your meeting with Major Azucena on the morning of the 30th of July, do you remember if you had a chance to tell her how you felt about working with Kempinski?

<8C-SU BAKOLA> It is done, Captain.

<Pol Asciak>: I did. That was, again, off the record. When I did, she explained that, given how serious and delicate the case seemed to be, she wanted her two best officers on board. On board and playing nice with one another is what she meant, I guess. She probably hoped that my being on the team would save her a headache or two.

<Elevii A. Tarkka ★☆☆>: "The best-laid plans of mice and men..."

<Pol Asciak>: [Nods gravely] Indeed.

<Elevii A. Tarkka ★☆☆>: Did the chief provide operational information concerning the investigation on that occasion?

<Pol Asciak>: [Pauses, appearing to think] Not much, if I remember correctly. She told me that Kempinski would be

taking care of my real briefing on this new case. Anyway, the meeting with Azucena was essentially a formality, just an opportunity for her to tick off the required administrative boxes.

<Elevii A. Tarkka ★☆☆>: Noted. And what did you do after that?

<Pol Asciak>: I did exactly what I was tasked with doing: I checked into the new case, took care of paperwork, and waited for Kempinski to show up. After lunch, I found him in his office with bloodshot eyes and wearing the same clothes he had on the previous night.

<Elevii A. Tarkka ★☆☆>: Go on.

<Pol Asciak>: I was surprised that he was with Deputy Satia, huddled behind a terminal screen, watching something together. Kempinski had an arm over Deputy Satia's shell and an ecstatic look on his face.

<Elevii A. Tarkka ★☆☆>: Could you try and further qualify why you were surprised?

<Pol Asciak>: Well, I guess I didn't expect Kempinski to be so physically comfortable with a Special Unit. You know, after our conversation the previous night...

<Elevii A. Tarkka ★☆☆>: Right. Do you know what they were watching so intently?

<Pol Asciak>: No idea. From the door, I could only see the back of his terminal display. It being Kempinski, it was probably a dogfight, a bikini mud wrestling match, or something of the sort.

<Merel Asciak>: [Appearing upset] Pol!

<Pol Asciak>: [Appearing surprised] What?!

<Merel Asciak>: [Speaking to Tarkka] Captain, I... I would like to request a break, if possible.

<Elevii A. Tarkka ★☆☆>: It is of course your legal right to do so, Miss Asciak. And while we are at it, I myself would

> like some extra time to follow up on a few things that were mentioned in this session. As it is almost lunchtime, would it be acceptable to both of you to stop here for the day and continue tomorrow?
>
> <Pol Asciak>: [Crossing his arms] Hrmph!
>
> <Merel Asciak>: [Speaking to Tarkka] I have something planned for the morning, so I'd appreciate it if we could meet tomorrow afternoon.

We agreed to resume the deposition the following day at 1 PM. After Pol and Merel Asciak left the interview room, I asked Deputy Bakola to retrieve the information concerning the Vannevar case from the station's mainframe and save it to our shared repository. The case files I was interested in included the complete recordings Deputy Satia had uploaded over the last two weeks.

After a quick lunch, Bakola and I started going through Deputy Satia's feed. ~~Interestingly enough, as it turns out, the field deputy and the Special Unit were indeed watching a vicious bikini mud-wrestling match.~~

INVESTIGATION DAY 4 (MORNING)

August 26 – SS8C

In the morning, I received a squeak-message from Major Azucena. ~~It was a thoughtful message, but it was also short and rather ungrammatical. It gave the impression of having been written in the interstice of time between other, presumably more pressing, responsibilities. The squeak simply said that she looked forward to hearing my thoughts on the book, if I ever found the time and the interest to read it.~~ On the topic of Vannevar and the irregularity of his profile, Major Azucena's squeak advised me not to worry about Vannevar for now. After all, his deposition was still a few days away, she wrote, before going on to reassure me that she would look into the matter of his profile herself as soon as possible.

Special Unit Deputy Bakola and I spent the first several hours of my fourth day of work in Sector 8C reviewing some of the video evidence that we had agreed to bring up during this afternoon's session. In one of those videos—an extract taken from the footage that the little automaton recorded from inside a ventilation duct—a tall, distinguished man enters the scene from the blurry left margin of the camera's field of view. Walking behind him is another man with a knife attached to his belt. The facial recognition software informs the viewer of the name of the second man via an interface overlay, with a special checkmark next to his name signifying that his digital records are available in full. Neither the name nor the criminal background of this man is particularly relevant to the present case, however. What matters is that he carries a taser electroshock weapon in his hand, and the device looks exactly like those used by field security officers.

At the center of the service automaton shot is a crudely plastered portion of the warehouse wall. Positioned in front of this section of the wall is a black leather couch that looks pristine and expensive. It provides a pleasant contrast to the rest of the space, which looks cluttered and dirty. The man carrying the taser uses the device to crudely direct the tall man to the couch. You can wait here, his body language growls, but don't try anything funny.

A dozen bulky old paper books are piled haphazardly next to the couch. On top of the pile of books are two statuettes representing crouched human figures. A reinforced metal door is cut off by the right edge of the camera's field of vision. The man with the taser walks to the metal door, knocks on it with the butt of the weapon, and waits.

The man on the couch is Egon Vannevar—there is no doubt about that. His height and facial features correspond to those of the man who was arrested in Satia's video, but the recognition software does not seem to be able to link his facial topography with a name or identity profile. A minute passes, and the software still cannot determine the identity of the tall man sitting on the couch. I pause the video and ask Deputy Bakola if they had any idea as to why that is the case. "Cases of missed identification can happen on occasion," the Special Unit explained, "especially when footage is captured from a point of view that is substantially above one's line of sight, as is the case here."

I remain unconvinced.

Nothing of note happens in the service automaton video for about a minute and a half. Then, a man walks out of the metal door on the right edge of the frame. The recognition software promptly identifies this new person as Hematsu Choksi. Choksi is a short, wiry man of South Asian descent. He wears a brightly colored sherwani and looks comically small next to Vannevar when the latter stands to shake Choksi's hand. The two talk for a while, but most of their dialogue is unintelligible because of the distance and the camera angle. Choksi nods and smiles, evidently pleased with the interaction. He then turns toward the man with the taser and makes a gesture. The armed man nods and leaves the warehouse through the metal door. Moments later, the same man returns, pushing a platform cart. On the cart is a brand-new LUNA shell: a latest-generation, matte-white, crab-like robotic body. The crustacean-inspired artifact appears to be lifeless on the cart, with its arms folded and its legs bent backward. In this pose, the shell has an almost perfectly prismatic shape.

Deputy Bakola paused the video at this point. "You might know this already," they said, "but what you are seeing here is a shell in its 'shipping configuration.' This pose allows a Special Unit to fit in a standard padded crate, which is of course optimal for storage. The fact that we see the LUNA in this pose likely indicates that the shell had been recently taken out of a container. My guess is that it had recently been shipped. It is possible that the shell was still vacant when this footage was recorded."

"Meaning that there is no... I mean, no organic—"

"Just an artificially intelligent shell, Captain. With no resident."

I nod and turn back toward the wall-sized screen. In the video, the man pushes the cart holding the robotic shell into roughly the center of the camera frame. Vannevar examines the external surface of the new LUNA closely. He says something to Choksi, who, in response, takes an electronic device out of his breast pocket and hands it to Vannevar. The latter man then unspools a filament-like cable out of one of the device's corners and plugs it into a precise spot in the gap between two of the metal plates of the shell. The screen of the device lights up. Vannevar brings it closer to its face, inspecting the readout of the link with the LUNA, and looks very satisfied with the readings. He detaches the filament-like cable from the shell and gives the device back to Choksi. The two shake hands. Not a single credit is exchanged, at least not in front of the camera.

<NOTE> Was the shell paid for in advance? Is Vannevar the terminus of this trade, or is he only a monomer within a longer molecule? </NOTE>

Choksi then gives a curt, polite nod and walks to the metal door. In a similarly unceremonious way, Vannevar gets behind the platform cart and pushes the LUNA shell out of the leftmost margin of the field of vision of the service droid. The man with the taser follows Vannevar with his hands in his pockets.

In Interview Room B2, Deputy Bakola stopped the video and switched to Satia's footage for July 30 with a timestamp they had previously set for our viewing: the recording of the three security officers' first informal joint meeting concerning the Vannevar case. The video takes place in the early afternoon, and Kempinski, Asciak, and Satia are sitting around a messy desk in Kempinski's office. They have just finished watching the same warehouse footage that Bakola and I had just examined. In Satia's video, Kempinski also pauses the video after Vannevar leaves the scene pushing the platform cart with a brand-new LUNA off camera. The field deputy turns toward Asciak and raises his eyebrows. His expression seems to ask "now you see what I mean?"

Satia also turn toward Asciak, who purses his lips and reluctantly admits that Kempinski is right—that part of the video should have set off some alarm bells.

"It damned well should have," the older officer replies raucously. Kempinski coughs into his elbow and then takes the service droid footage back to the point when Vannevar sits down on the warehouse sofa. "Yup, I guess we should count ourselves twice lucky," Kempinski says.

"Twice?" questions Deputy Satia's disembodied voice.

"First to have captured this stuff on video and second that it happened so early in the li'l crab's feed."

Kempinski is referring to the fact that this exchange could have easily passed unnoticed, given the amount of spectacularly incriminating evidence the little automaton witnessed in the three days of uninterrupted recording before its battery ran out.

<NOTE> To this day, I wonder whether anybody ever bothered to retrieve the little guy from that warehouse's ventilation duct. </NOTE>

Bakola and I went back to the video originally captured by the infiltrating automaton, going significantly beyond the point where Vannevar leaves the scene. Almost nothing happens in the following two hours of recorded footage, which we watched at twice the recorded speed. The sole exception, perhaps, is the return of the bald man with the taser about three minutes after he walks out of the frame with Vannevar. Upon returning, this man crosses the camera's view pushing the platform cart, now empty, back to the place from where he originally took it. His swift reappearance implies that the destination of the LUNA shell was probably not within walking distance, or Vannevar would likely have needed the cart for longer than three minutes. It is thus probable that an electric vehicle was waiting outside the warehouse to pick up Vannevar and the shell, or simply to collect the LUNA, and drive it elsewhere within the sector.

I asked Deputy Bakola if they knew how heavy that new shell model was. A squeak search performed by the Special Unit answered my question instantly. That particular LUNA weighs fifty-nine kilograms "dry," meaning without a nervous system and the various fluids—both organic and inorganic—necessary for its functioning. It could weigh over seventy kilograms if inhabited and fully operational. What that meant was that—without help or transport of some sort—one could not easily move such a shell around, or not very far anyway. With this information in mind, the obvious next step for any investigative team working on the case should have been to look for camera recordings in the area immediately surrounding the warehouse: droids, drones, traffic monitors, a Special Unit fortuitously patrolling the area... basically anything with video-capturing capabilities. Kempinski and Asciak knew the exact time of Vannevar's departure from the building; in our surveilled world, something or someone was bound to have seen him leave.

What We Owe the Dead

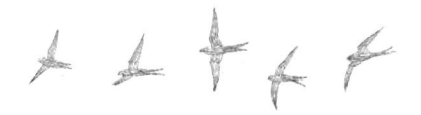

<NOTE> The following section should be removed. It has little to no relevance to the case. Re-read to make sure there is nothing of use to salvage. </NOTE>

Around mid-morning, I encouraged Deputy Bakola to take a couple of hours off to recharge in case they needed a break, recognizing that this afternoon's deposition session would be a long one.

After Bakola left, ~~I purchased a snack from the vending machine in the hall (B0). The door to Room B1, where I was introduced to Captain Kutta, is just next to the vending machine, so I noticed that the door was open. Determined to obtain a firmer hold on some of the details mentioned by Pol Asciak the previous day,~~ I decided to ask Uncle Rahman a couple of questions. ~~I did not have much time before the start of the new deposition session but decided to do this anyway, so I activated my LUNA's embedded audio-recording mode with a flick of my wrist, took a deep breath, and walked in.~~

> N.E. 330 – August 26, 11:12:11
> [ELEVII'S LUNA - Kh31r 1.2(R)] Audio201
> (text automatically generated from audio)
>
> <Elevii A. Tarkka ★☆☆>: Knock, knock.
>
> <Rahman Kutta ★☆☆>: Who's there?
>
> <Elevii A. Tarkka ★☆☆>: May I come in, Captain?
>
> <Rahman Kutta ★☆☆>: Elevii, I'm so glad to see you! Please take a seat.
> [Pauses] How can I be of service? Oh, and have you seen the swallows this morning?
>
> <Elevii A. Tarkka ★☆☆>: The swallows? I... I cannot say that I have. You see, we've been examining some footage on the big screen all morning. A waste of a great view, I know.
> [Pauses] What's new in the bird world?

<Rahman Kutta ★☆☆>: Oh, you know, it is that time of the year. Swallows are flying in bigger and bigger swoops, and their forays are taking them farther and farther away from the sanctuaries. I would not be surprised to see most of them leave within a week or so.

<Elevii A. Tarkka ★☆☆>: Leave?

<Rahman Kutta ★☆☆>: As in migrate.

<Elevii A. Tarkka ★☆☆>: I am not sure I follow, Captain.

<Rahman Kutta ★☆☆>: Golly, what do they teach kids in school these days?

<NOTE> The automatic transcript of the audio recording was unfortunately not sensitive enough to pick up the grinding of my teeth. </NOTE>

<Rahman Kutta ★☆☆>: Our beloved birds will be flying to the other side of the world soon. Most will stop on the northern coast of the North American continent. Some will go as far as Greenland.

<Elevii A. Tarkka ★☆☆>: All the way to HOOS-MING FOUR?!

<Rahman Kutta ★☆☆>: Most certainly! And they need to pack their bags before the hot season sets in. If they stay too long, the temperature will become so high that they will be unable to survive the flight.

<Elevii A. Tarkka ★☆☆>: Whoa, how do th—

<Rahman Kutta ★☆☆>: [Interrupting] They will pass by HOOS-MING TWO, just a day of flying north of here, and then they will head for the Andes... and eventually follow the Rockies. They will fly at night, finding shelter from the daytime heat in mountain caves and crevices, filling their bellies with whatever they manage to find on our scorched little planet.
[Pauses] Oh, and, on the topic of food, could I tempt you with some homemade cookies? Mushroom flour. My wife makes them!

<Elevii A. Tarkka ★☆☆>: Thanks, but no. I will, however, take you up on your *other* offer, if that's okay.

<Rahman Kutta ★☆☆>: Which other offer?

<Elevii A. Tarkka ★☆☆>: The other day, you said I could come to you whenever I needed help. And, well, here I am.

<Rahman Kutta ★☆☆>: Oh, I see! You need a hand. [Chuckles] See what I did there? A hand! [Winks twice] It's a joke!

<Elevii A. Tarkka ★☆☆>: [Appearing unfazed] Sure. I get it. [Nods] Great.

<Rahman Kutta ★☆☆>: But seriously, I'm not sure this old dog can teach you any new tricks.

<Elevii A. Tarkka ★☆☆>: It is not new tricks I'm after, Captain. Nor detailed accounts of swallow behavior, although I can see why this is a fascinating topic for you. [Takes a deep breath] I'm here to ask a couple of questions related to the case I'm working.

<Rahman Kutta ★☆☆>: By all means, ask away.

<Elevii A. Tarkka ★☆☆>: So—

<Rahman Kutta ★☆☆>: [Interrupting] Speaking of your case, did I tell you I met that nice young woman in the hall the other day. What is her name... you know, Pol's sister.

<Elevii A. Tarkka ★☆☆>: Merel Asciak.

<Rahman Kutta ★☆☆>: Yes, Merel. Isn't she terrific?

<Elevii A. Tarkka ★☆☆>: [Appearing unfazed] Okay, I want to ask about *Duplicate Conduit*, a game with which I believe you must have some familiarity.

I purposefully looked at the issue of *Cond-Passion* magazine lying open on his desk. The cover of this particular issue celebrated Onfime Mumbi, a *Conduit* hall of famer who had recently retired from the competitive scene.

<Elevii A. Tarkka ★☆☆>: Specifically, I'm interested in the game's origins. Could you help me understand why anyone would refer to *Duplicate Conduit* as something that was "discovered"?

<Rahman Kutta ★☆☆>: Oh, this is an easy one! See that promotional flyer on my door? "Explore the original syphon megatower" and all the rest?

<Elevii A. Tarkka ★☆☆>: Yes.

<Rahman Kutta ★☆☆>: And you know about those puzzling remains at the foot of our glorious cooling megatower?

<Elevii A. Tarkka ★☆☆>: [Turns back to Kutta] You mean the alien wreck?

<Rahman Kutta ★☆☆>: Oh, they *do* teach something useful in school after all!

<Elevii A. Tarkka ★☆☆>: Well, I know it was identified as a large-ish transport vehicle of an advanced alien civilization that landed in Antarctica. Or crashed here. Hard to say exactly, as that was a few million years ago.

<Rahman Kutta ★☆☆>: Thirty-five million years ago, to be precise. That was before this continent was buried in kilometers of ice.

<Elevii A. Tarkka ★☆☆>: Right. And when the ice came, it squeezed the alien ship and pushed it around for a very, very long time. So, when the polar caps eventually melted, all that was left was little more than crushed remains. That is what we found—a barely recognizable husk. I guess that's why they call it the most boring first contact story ever told.

<Rahman Kutta ★☆☆>: It might be boring to some, sure... but can you imagine how the crew working on the foundations of the tower must have felt when they found an alien artifact half-buried in the Antarctic soil?

<Elevii A. Tarkka ★☆☆>: I mean, don't get me wrong, Rahman, this is all fascinating stuff from a historical point of view, but what does it all have to do with *Conduit*?

<Rahman Kutta ★☆☆>: Well, the unearthing of the remains of the Fleeting ship was not the complete letdown you've just described. As it turned out, a portion of its hull was still in one piece, relatively speaking. It was twisted and broken, but it survived the landing, the ice, and the passage of time.

<Elevii A. Tarkka ★☆☆>: If memory serves me right, it contained the remains of an alien cafeteria of sorts. Right? Or was it a kitchen?

<Rahman Kutta ★☆☆>: Whatever its function was, it was from there that our archeologists retrieved a container that remained miraculously intact. And, in that sealed box, they found a few scrolls made of a polymer not entirely unlike our postplastic. They were covered in squiggly Fleeting writing.

At this point in our conversation, my hand lit up and vibrated slightly. I was being notified of ~~a squeak-message from my mother,~~ something that did not require my immediate attention, ~~to be sure,~~ but it captured Uncle Rahman's attention and derailed his train of thought.

<Rahman Kutta ★☆☆>: Ahem... wh— where was I?

<Elevii A. Tarkka ★☆☆>: Squiggly writings on alien scrolls.

<Rahman Kutta ★☆☆>: Ah, yes! Well, within a year, a team of our best linguists decoded what was written on the Fleeting scrolls, with the help of some artificial intelligence tools. The scrolls turned out to be handbooks for the maintenance and repair of a few of the spaceship's systems. The information extracted from those scrolls spurred the development of a number of new inventions that make our lives possible today. Think of squeak technology and geno-sequencing.

<Elevii A. Tarkka ★☆☆>: Oh...

<Rahman Kutta ★☆☆>: But one of the scrolls in the box was a little different from the others, in that it was a different color. That one, too, was a technical manual of sorts. Unlike the others, though, that special scroll detailed

the procedures and rules for playing a tabletop game called something like "Manifold Passage"—or "Giving Forward in More Ways than One," depending on which Fleeting translation you accept.

<Elevii A. Tarkka ★☆☆>: Are you telling me we found the rules for *Duplicate Conduit* in an alien refrigerator of sorts?

<Rahman Kutta ★☆☆>: [Chuckles] Not quite, no. What they found on that scroll was not the rules for *Duplicate Conduit* as we know it today. The text did offer a complete description of a game's rules and necessary equipment, but playing the game as the Fleeting did would require an understanding of their traditions and social norms that was not part of the rulebook. To use a linguistic analogy, we found the game's "grammar" but not the vocabulary necessary to play.
[Pauses] We know that theirs is a highly metaphorical language. It's basically impossible to understand what the Fleeting are referring to without being part of their culture. We do not know what mythical event or famous historical figure is being alluded to, let alone their specific way of understanding the meaning behind that.

<Elevii A. Tarkka ★☆☆>: And the manuals we found were not enough to put together a general view of who they were and what they believed in?

<Rahman Kutta ★☆☆>: We could put together parts of it... but, as they say, we couldn't derive the entire lion from its claw.

<NOTE> This statement of course made me think of the fact that the geno-sequenced material that we have managed to save from extinct species is precisely what gives us hope that one day animals will walk this planet again. Our plan literally involves bringing lions back by rebuilding them from a few scraps of genetic material. </NOTE>

<Rahman Kutta ★☆☆>: And so, the game we currently play as *Duplicate Conduit* is inevitably different from what we originally found. What we have today is an attempt to make sense of an alien tradition by loosely adapting it to the context of human society. Does that make sense?

<Elevii A. Tarkka ★☆☆>: Somewhat. [Pauses] And do we know how the rules for a tabletop game ended up in a crate full of mission-critical information on a spaceship?

<Rahman Kutta ★☆☆>: I guess it must have been pretty important for the Fleeting, or it might have just fallen in there by mistake. We might never find out.

<Elevii A. Tarkka ★☆☆>: I see.

<Rahman Kutta ★☆☆>: And that's how *Duplicate Conduit*, one of the world's most popular pastimes, can be considered a *discovered* game, rather than one that was *designed*. Although, as I have tried to explain, the game can also be considered both things at the same time, in a way.

<Elevii A. Tarkka ★☆☆>: Well, thank you fo—

<Rahman Kutta ★☆☆>: [Interrupting] Should you be interested in knowing more about this, I would recommend the work of Grace Tizzi. She has written a couple of books on the history and development of the current design of *Duplicate Conduit*, and she has a regular column in *Cond-Passion* magazine.

Captain Kutta gestured toward the other end of his desk, where a magazine lay open.

<Elevii A. Tarkka ★☆☆>: Tizzi, huh? I am sure I've heard that name before...

<NOTE> I indeed had read her name the day before in the process of examining Kempinski's security profile. Grace Tizzi, a full professor at the University of Byrgius (on the moon), is one of the world's leading game scholars, who also happens to be the former wife of my case's victim. </NOTE>

<Rahman Kutta ★☆☆>: Have you watched feeds from ranked tournaments of *Conduit*? If you have, then you may have seen her providing live commentary on the matches. Situational analyses, strategic outlooks, things like that.

<Elevii A. Tarkka ★☆☆>: I don't think I've ever seen that.

In any case, Captain, this was very useful. And thorough. Many thanks.

<Rahman Kutta ★☆☆>: Happy to be useful. Is that all?

<Elevii A. Tarkka ★☆☆>: Yes, that's all. Now I'd better go and grab something to eat before this afternoon's session.

I stood up and walked to the door. Instead of leaving immediately, I stopped in front of the tourist flyer that Kutta referenced during our conversation.

<Elevii A. Tarkka ★☆☆>: Captain. One more thing, if I may...

<Rahman Kutta ★☆☆>: Sure.

<Elevii A. Tarkka ★☆☆>: Someone drew some funny angels around the megatower there, and I wondered...

<Rahman Kutta ★☆☆>: [Interrupting] Ah, yes! That was my granddaughter—Kety, short for Ketereth. Loves to doodle.
[Pauses] Those are... well, that is a bit of a long story.

<Elevii A. Tarkka ★☆☆>: Never mind. Maybe something for the next time?

<Rahman Kutta ★☆☆>: Elevii, do you know who built HOOS-MING ONE?

<Elevii A. Tarkka ★☆☆>: I— it was mostly droids, wasn't it?

<Rahman Kutta ★☆☆>: Mostly, yes. Well, in case you want to know more about those angels, as you called them, I'd suggest you look up the bird people.

<Elevii A. Tarkka ★☆☆>: The bird people?

<Rahman Kutta ★☆☆>: Yeah. A squeak search would be enough to start.

I nodded, promised that I would look them up, and finally managed to excuse myself.

That night, after having dinner in my hotel room, I decided to fulfill my promise to Captain Kutta. I squeak-searched for information concerning the bird people, and this is what I found:

In the early phases of the construction of the first megatower, droid technology was still prohibitively expensive. At the time, the automata's abilities were better suited for repetitive and heavy labor than for tasks requiring finesse. This limited their initial use to the digging of the foundations of HOOS-MING ONE and jobs such as the transportation and laying of pipes or the housings for the ammonia tanks at the base of the thermo-syphon. Fleeting-inspired technological breakthroughs in robotics changed the situation in the decades that followed, when robots took over essentially all manual labor, enabling the rapid completion of the megatower.

But in the early stages of development of HOOS-MING ONE, most construction jobs were typically performed hanging several kilometers above the Antarctic soil, and this labor was the exclusive domain of human workers. Climate migrants from Southeast Asia, desperate to survive and secure a future for their children, accepted employment building the megatower in conditions that it would no longer be morally or legally acceptable for humans or any T3 artificial intelligences to work under. The life expectancy of these workers was of course shockingly low, and work-related deaths were in the tens of thousands before the droids took over.

There are a few folk tales, mostly shared among people of Pakistani and Indian heritage, recounting the story of the humans who constructed the tower during these early years. According to these stories, after years working on miles-high scaffolding and hanging from harnesses, some of the workers managed to do the impossible: they learned to breathe the thin air of the stratosphere and tame the turbulent winds that howl outside HOOS-MING ONE. Spending the best part of their days among the swallows, these workers eventually learned how to glide, and eventually to fly. Free like the birds, the dark-skinned men and women soared away and never returned to the tower.

There is another and almost opposite myth that accounts for construction workers who did not return home from a day of work. This parallel legend talks about men who, instead of growing wings, turned completely into swallows. Unlike the first kind of birdmen, the ones who transformed into swallows did not leave HOOS-MING ONE for good, but rather come back every year, autumn after autumn, continuing to visit their friends and relatives.

What We Owe the Dead

INVESTIGATION DAY 4 (AFTERNOON)

August 26 – SS8C

File ID: KC04
N.E. 330 – August 26, 13:02
[8C-SU Bakola (6584AR-4)]
(text automatically generated from video)

<Elevii A. Tarkka ★☆☆>: This is the second day of Mister Asciak's deposition concerning his involvement in the Vannevar case. It is part of the evidentiary body of the internal investigation I am conducting. The date is August the 26th, 330. It is just after one o'clock in the afternoon. Also present at this deposition is Mister Asciak's legal representative—Merel Asciak.
[Speaking to Pol Asciak] Are you ready to continue? Shall we proceed?

<Pol Asciak>: Well, that is why we're all here, isn't it?

<Elevii A. Tarkka ★☆☆>: [Speaking to Pol Asciak] Mister Asciak, yesterday morning you were telling us about your first meeting with Field Deputy Kempinski in the context of

the Vannevar investigation. That was on the 30th of July.

<Pol Asciak>: [Nods] The afternoon of the 30th, yes. The day after the station party.

<Elevii A. Tarkka ★☆☆>: On that occasion, when you walked in, Kempinski and Special Unit Deputy Satia were watching something on a terminal screen. What happened after that?

<Pol Asciak>: Well, I guess I informed Kempinski that I had indeed been officially assigned to the case.

<Elevii A. Tarkka ★☆☆>: Was it Kempinski who notified you that Deputy Satia were also part of the—and I am quoting you from yesterday's session—"unlikely investigative team?"

<Pol Asciak>: I believe so.
[Pauses] Yes. Thinking about it now, I'm not sure why the boss didn't mention Satia's involvement. It must have slipped her mind.
[Shrugs] In any case, I was ready to start working the case. I was even ready to lead it, as the highest-ranking officer involved.

<Elevii A. Tarkka ★☆☆>: And yet you didn't raise the topic of leadership or rank. At least not on that occasion.

<Pol Asciak>: Not on that occasion, no. The matter came up a few days later, though. On the day before the accident. [Pauses] Kempinski and I were in a cruiser on our way back from the moon, and we... well, we had an argument about how the case was going. About the need for mutual trust and shared objectives.

<Elevii A. Tarkka ★☆☆>: Noted, and we'll get to that, eventually. For now, if you don't mind, let's go back to Kempinski's office on the afternoon of the 30th.

<Pol Asciak>: Sure.
[Scratches his chin] Well, as he promised he would, Stan introduced me to the case by showing me a segment of the service android video that I had submitted as evidence for my previous case.

<Elevii A. Tarkka ★☆☆>: The Choksi investigation.

<Pol Asciak>: Right. I remember he took his sweet time, too. He started with some small talk, and then he offered me some snacks... he even left the office for a while—not sure to do what. When Kempinski came back, he spun his terminal screen around and played the first seven or eight minutes of the warehouse video.

<Elevii A. Tarkka ★☆☆>: You're referring to the part where Vannevar—if that is his real name—receives a new LUNA shell from Choksi?

<Pol Asciak>: Correct.

<Elevii A. Tarkka ★☆☆>: What I want to focus on is the conversation that ensued from your watching—or rather re-watching—that scene together with Kempinski. I hope you don't mind if we review that through Deputy Satia's recording of the exchange.

<Pol Asciak>: [Frowns] Really? [Appearing annoyed] I mean, are we going to dissect every single interaction that Kempinski and I had throughout the case?

<Elevii A. Tarkka ★☆☆>: Inspector Asciak... [Correcting herself] Mister Asciak: I believe we're working toward the same goal here. We both aim to reach a thorough and unambiguous understanding of what happened during the final phases of the Vannevar investigation. Don't you agree?

<Pol Asciak>: [Appearing frustrated] Of course I agree. All I'm saying is that, at this pace, we're going to be stuck in limbo for a whole damn month! Why don't—

<Merel Asciak>: [Interrupting] That's enough, Pol! [Speaking to Tarkka] Captain, I apologize for my client's tone and unfortunate choice of words. May I request a brief break so that I may speak privately with him?

<Elevii A. Tarkka ★☆☆>: [Nods] You certainly may. But before that, let me reassure you both that this deposition will only take a few days. Four or five at the most. That said,

it is imperative that I have the facts straight. [Speaking to Pol Asciak] There are a couple of points in the conversation we're about to watch that I need to review with you before we can move forward. Now, would 20 minutes be enough for your...
[Tilts her head slightly to the side] private discussion?

\<Merel Asciak\>: That will be plenty, thank you.

\<Pol Asciak\>: [Inaudible]

The Asciaks then left the room with Pol silently shaking his head. After they closed the door behind them, ~~I unwrapped the vending machine snack that I had hastily repackaged after failing to finish it after my unintentionally extended conversation with Uncle Rahman. While finishing my meal,~~ I asked Deputy Bakola what they thought about Pol Asciak's behavior. At the time, I had not yet told the Special Unit about the informal ~~and rather shocking~~ admission of guilt that Asciak had volunteered just before our first deposition session. However, it was obvious from their answer that they understood where I was coming from and saw that I was still unable to make sense of Asciak's seemingly irrational conduct. Deputy Bakola offered their point of view, starting from the observation that Asciak had displayed certain obsessive personality traits throughout his career, which are particularly evident in his perfectionism and conscientious adherence to rules and protocols. This disposition, the Special Unit continued, is generally in line with an individual experiencing high anxiety and the need to feel in control of their situation.

According to Deputy Bakola, what had happened to Asciak over the past three weeks must be difficult to deal with. In response, Asciak had progressively lost his grip on things: first his case, then his emotions, and finally his career. In support of their interpretation of the available information, the Special Unit added that the presence of a new girlfriend likely also functioned as a catalyst for the stress to become overwhelming. To clarify what they meant, Bakola quoted an Old Era literary figure.

\<NOTE\> I recovered the complete quote from Oscar Wilde, which I am copying in this note. "It is always painful to part from people whom one has known for a very brief space of time. The absence of old friends, one can endure with equanimity. But even a momentary separation from anyone to whom one has just been introduced is almost unbearable." (Cecily in *The Importance of Being Earnest*) </NOTE>

~~What intrigued me about Deputy Bakola's analysis of Asciak's behavior was not their detailed (albeit somewhat obvious) psychological profiling, but rather their revealing a glimmer of something new about themselves: a dimension of Bakola that was extraneous to their professional role.~~ I nodded and thanked Deputy Bakola. ~~Lost in thought, I finished my lunch before making up my mind to ask the Special Unit for permission to speak off the record. Nodding in that endearing way Special Units do, repeatedly tilting their entire body up and down, Bakola consented to my request. "Do you have a specific interest in Old Era literature?" I asked. They replied that they enjoyed reading old books in their spare time. I rummaged in my bag and produced the copy of *Antigone* that I had received earlier that morning. "Do you happen to know anything about this one?" They immediately recognized it. "Of course!" they exclaimed. "That's an Old Era classic!" Encouraged by their enthusiastic reaction, I ventured to ask if they had any opinions about that book. Their answer puzzled me. To paraphrase, they basically stated that it depended on who I was asking: the cyborg officer or just the biological woman."~~

Before the Asciaks returned to the interview room, I also had time to send a quick update to Major Azucena informing her that the second day of Asciak's deposition was proceeding according to schedule. Upon returning to Room B2, Pol Asciak seemed calmer. Once everyone around the table was ready to continue, I launched the portion of Satia's footage that would be the focus of this afternoon's deposition. The lights in the room progressively dimmed, and a bidimensional rendition of Pol Asciak started to materialize on the wall-sized screen. In the video, it is the afternoon of July 30th, and Asciak is leaning back in a chair in Kempinski's office.

"What can I say?" the projected version of Inspector Asciak concedes, "You were right. This should have set off some alarm bells."

"It damned well should have," Kempinski replies. Then the older officer coughs into his elbow and reverses footage back to the point when Vannevar sits down on the couch in Choksi's warehouse. "Yup, I guess we should count ourselves twice lucky," he adds.

"Twice?" ask Deputy Satia.

"First to have captured this stuff on video at all and second that it happened so early in the li'l crab's feed. To be fair," Kempinski continues, "I would probably have missed it too if it hadn't been right at the beginning of the recording and... well, if it weren't for this guy." Kempinski pushes his index finger against the screen causing the image to become slightly distorted.

"What about him?" Asciak asks with an inquisitive expression.

"He... you know, bub, grabbed my attention. It was... a gut feeling, I guess" Kempinski replied.

"Doing investigative work based on unexplained hunches. Really? Have we stooped that low?"

"What else should I call it? A misplaced sense of familiarity that warranted a second look? Maybe that works better for you."

"Don't get me wrong, Kempinski, I'm very happy you did take that second look. Still, hunches in the year 330? Come on!"

In the video, Deputy Satia take advantage of the moment of silence that follows Asciak's exclamation to speak up. The Special Unit's body language indicates that they have missed something and are confused, probably unable to keep up with their more experienced human colleagues. "Apologies, officers," they say tentatively, "but we are not sure that we are following. We are unable to detect any illegal behavior in the footage we have all just watched. Correction: the bald man is holding a taser, which is indeed a felony."

"You're right about the taser, Deputy," Asciak replies.

"In a perfect world, crooks wouldn't walk around wielding police enforcement tools." "In that perfect world, the three of us would be out of a job," Kempinski adds dryly.

<Elevii A. Tarkka ★☆☆>: [Pauses the video] Let's stop here for a moment.

> [Speaking to Pol Asciak] Of course, Satia are right to bring up the issue of the taser. Was that weapon traced back to the corrupt security officers you arrested?
>
> <Pol Asciak>: It certainly was. The tasers in the warehouse all came from 79B. The two bad apples I caught were involved in Choksi's operations in a number of ways, including weapons embezzlement. You can find all of that in my final report, in case you need more information.
>
> <Elevii A. Tarkka ★☆☆>: And what did you make of Kempinski's mentioning a "sense of familiarity" regarding the man on the couch? I'm referring to the man we now know as Egon Vannevar.
>
> <Pol Asciak>: I didn't make much of it at the time. I guess I suspected he might be pretending to be following a hunch to avoid having to confess something even more embarrassing.
>
> <Elevii A. Tarkka ★☆☆>: Noted. [Pauses] Is it okay if we continue watching, or are there comments or other information you would like to add before we resume?
>
> <Pol Asciak>: I have nothing to add. If I recall correctly, the next part of the conversation is pretty self-explanatory.
>
> <Elevii A. Tarkka ★☆☆>: [Turns toward the screen and resumes the video with a gesture of her LUNA hand]

Deputy Satia's point of view tilts to one side: The Special Unit are still waiting for their answer. "So, what constituted an infringement of the law in the footage we have just watched?"

Kempinski raises his eyebrows and turns toward Asciak, who nods resolutely to indicate that he accepts the responsibility of explaining. "As you know better than either of us," Asciak says to Deputy Satia, "it is practically impossible to steal a shell or kidnap a cyborg."

Satia perform the distinctive Special Unit nod, showing agreement and appearing eager to help the conversation progress.

"Chances are, then," Asciak continues, "that the LUNA in the video was not stolen property. Let's consider another possibility, then.

Let's imagine a hypothetical scenario where a buyer has the kind of chips required to purchase that shell. Now, would such a person buy a latest-gen LUNA in a disreputable warehouse known for its black-market stunts?"

"It would be illogical to legally purchase it there. We see," reply Deputy Satia.

<Elevii A. Tarkka ★☆☆>: [Pauses the video] [Speaking to Pol Asciak] You mentioned that a shell cannot be stolen or kidnapped. I know they have security features like location tracking and self-protection capabilities even when they are without a... [Appearing to hesitate] ...a resident. Are you referring to those features?

<Pol Asciak>: Modern shells have internal tracking and systems meant to ensure their own integrity and safety. Those systems cannot be accessed or modified from outside the shell itself, meaning that these critical features are impervious to remote hacks and can only be disabled by taking the shell itself apart.

<Elevii A. Tarkka ★☆☆>: Could you explain what would prevent a smuggler from doing just that? I mean finding a way inside the exoskeleton?

<Pol Asciak>: [Gestures to Bakola] Deputy?

<Self ☆>: [Speaking to Tarkka] Permission to speak, Captain?

<Elevii A. Tarkka ★☆☆>: Granted, of course.

<Self ☆>: Like most droids above a threshold level of sentience, cyborgs will do whatever it takes to avoid being breached. Once the inside of the shell is exposed, cyborgs are completely defenseless against physical damage. Even if no harm were intended, being exposed to a non-sterile environment would still be extremely dangerous to us because of our lack of a proper immune system. In short, such a breach would be a serious existential threat, and a cyborg would fight tooth and nail to prevent that from happening.

<Elevii A. Tarkka ★☆☆>: And in the case of an empty shell?

<Self ☆>: Even without a biological resident, the T3 intelligence of a modern shell is able to act in self-defense when detecting a threat to its integrity. A shell can even self-destruct to avoid an unauthorized breach. As a deterrent, each of us contains enough explosives to guarantee a lose-lose outcome for anyone attempting to capture or incapacitate us.

<Elevii A. Tarkka ★☆☆>: Fascinating. [Pauses] Do these preventive measures work? I mean, what numbers are we talking about?

<Pol Asciak>: Last time I checked, not a single missing shell has been reported in the past 31 years.

<Self ☆>: 32.

<NOTE> I remember wondering how many shells—with or without an organic resident—had decided to blow themselves up over the same period. Of course, I did not consider asking such a question, given the nature of the situation and the likelihood that such a topic would make Deputy Bakola uncomfortable. This information was easily accessible on the public networks, however, and the number is two. </NOTE>

<Elevii A. Tarkka ★☆☆>: [Nods] [Draws in a long breath] Well, that was enlightening. Thank you both. [Takes the video back a few seconds and resumes playing it]

"...would such a person buy a latest-gen LUNA in a disreputable warehouse known for its black-market stunts?"

"It would be illogical to legally purchase it there. We see. The fact that we are not witnessing a purchase, then," continues the disembodied voice of Deputy Satia, "is also consistent with the fact that no money or goods of equivalent value seem to have been exchanged between the two men."

"At least not on camera, anyway," adds Asciak.

"But if we assume that the LUNA in the video was not stolen, and if what we witnessed was not a sale of some sort," the Special Unit inquire, "then what did we just watch? What were those men doing?"

At this point, the inspector explains that what worries both him and Kempinski is not the lawfulness of the men's behavior so much as the implications of their actions. "If we exclude the illegal sale scenario," continues Asciak, "then we are left with only one possibility: this was a handover."

"Right," Kempinski finally intervenes, "and if this is a back-alley handover, then there's no doubt as to whether what they're doing is illegal. Someone doesn't want to be identified as the recipient of this shell or doesn't want the shell to go through customs and inter-sector checks. Maybe both."

Deputy Satia process this new information. After a few seconds, they say, "Let me see if we understand what you are saying, gentlemen. As we have seen, the shell in the video was arranged in shipping configuration. Given that and its brand-new appearance, it is likely that this shell was vacant at the time. A person somewhere bought a shell and then sent it to our sector."

"Or they already owned it and wanted to sell it in this sector without going through customs and security checks," Asciak comments.

"We see. So, once those checks and taxes have been successfully dodged," the Special Unit continue, "that same someone goes and collects it, either in person or through an intermediary."

"Yes, it would be inconvenient, awkward, and probably very expensive," adds Kempinski, "but that's the kind of price someone might be willing to pay not to answer any questions."

> <Elevii A. Tarkka ★☆☆>: [Pauses the video] Would you care to add any comments on what we've just watched?
>
> <Pol Asciak>: Not particularly, no.
>
> <Elevii A. Tarkka ★☆☆>: Then I'm going to progress the video to a later part of this conversation. In the segment

I am about to show you, Deputy Satia ask Field Deputy Kempinski about the next step in the team's investigation.

<Pol Asciak>: Okay.

<Elevii A. Tarkka ★☆☆>: The question, again, was directed toward Kempinski, but you were the one who answered it. Let's take a look.

Crouching on a chair in Kempinski's office, Deputy Satia turn their body slightly toward Kempinski. The old officer pops a pill in his mouth, takes an unassuming small bottle from one of his desk drawers, and gulps down something to wash the pill down his throat.

"If your hypothesis is correct," Satia ask, "how can we find out who bought that LUNA and why it was sent to Sector 8C as if it were contraband?"

Inspector Asciak responds as Kempinski hits his own chest repeatedly with an open hand, apparently attempting to dislodge the pill he has just swallowed.

"We have two paths before us," Asciak explains. "The first is tracking down the tall man, presumably by means of public surveillance cameras outside the warehouse. The other path leads us to the detention facility a few stories above our heads to see what else we can squeeze out of that parasite Choksi."

"Can we not do both?" Satia ask excitedly.

"One does not exclude the other, but my preference would be to try to identify the recipient of the shell first and then talk to Choksi. The more we know about the other man, the less likely it is that Choksi will succeed in taking us for a ride."

Kempinski finally manages to swallow the pill. Relieved, he gasps for air, takes a long breath, and then says, barely audibly, "Egon Vannevar."

"What was that?" asks Asciak.

"Name's Egon Vannevar." Kempinski is still having some trouble breathing. "The tall man's name."

Asciak looks surprised. He probably had not expected this level of efficiency from his older colleague. "Okay, I'm impressed, Field Deputy! Care to share how you found out?"

"Security cameras, like you said. Around the time the tall man left the building, an automated van passed by the warehouse. It looked like the kind of vehicle you might need to move a shell around. Property of SELENIC—the company logo was printed all over the van."

Kempinski takes another ragged breath and finally says, "From there, it wasn't hard to identify who ordered and paid for the ride."

"Did you have to go to SELENIC in person for that?"

"I did. I was already in the area the other day. It was... convenient, let's say."

Asciak scratches his right cheek. "Egon Vannevar, huh? I don't think I've heard that name before."

"Well, the profile for this guy stinks to high heaven, and that name is almost certainly fake, which is a bummer, of course. Chances are, though, that Choksi only knows him by that name, too."

"Gotcha. You think we could still play this card? I mean asking him about Vannevar?"

"Not much to lose by trying, I guess."

> <Elevii A. Tarkka ★☆☆>: [Pauses the video] Mister Asciak, did the irregularities that Field Deputy Kempinski identified in Vannevar's security profile trouble you at the time?
>
> <Pol Asciak>: If you've talking about the entire profile likely being bogus, obviously I was concerned. More than troubling me, though, those anomalies confirmed that whatever was under the stone that Kempinski had turned was worth a closer look.
>
> <Elevii A. Tarkka ★☆☆>: And did it bother you that Kempinski had started working on the case independently before the investigation was officially sanctioned?
>
> <Pol Asciak>: I'm not sure I understand your question.

<Elevii A. Tarkka ★☆☆>: Did you feel apprehensive about working with Kempinski? Did the fact that he had more information than you did at this point in the case make you distrustful of him?

<Pol Asciak>: Look, Kempinski and I had our differences, but I didn't feel territorial about the Choksi case. Or its continuation, for that matter. I... with his reputation, I was surprised that he had taken it upon himself to do some of the preliminary groundwork. But, no, I didn't doubt him or his intentions at the time.

<8C-SU BAKOLA>: *Asciak is lying.*

<Pol Asciak>: What I'm trying to say is that I took both his interest in the case and the information he provided at face value.

<ELEVII'S LUNA>: *What do you mean?*

<Pol Asciak>: Does that answer your question?

<8C-SU BAKOLA>: *We can prove he was suspicious of Kempinski right from the beginning.*

<Pol Asciak>: Captain?

<Elevii A. Tarkka ★☆☆>: I... y-yes, sorry. Your... it doesn't matter. Let's move on to one more event I'd like to review form the same afternoon.

<Pol Asciak>: [Appearing mildly annoyed] Sure.

<8C-SU BAKOLA>: *Later that evening, Asciak searched for a video of Kempinski visiting SELENIC's local administrative offices. We are looking at the queries in the security mainframe linked to his profile.*

<ELEVII'S LUNA>: *Did he find one? Is there a video of Kempinski at SELENIC?*

<8C-SU BAKOLA>: *We are still reviewing the results. Hang on.*

I advanced Satia's footage about half an hour to a point in the video that I had preliminarily marked for discussion. The setting of this new extract is a corridor of Security Station 8C (Floor A). Inspector Asciak and Deputy Satia have just left Field Deputy Kempinski's office and are walking next to one another.

From the station's records, I know that Asciak and Satia have worked as partners on several occasions before this case. The tone of their conversation is friendly and informal. After some small talk, Asciak asks Satia how they are feeling about the new case. Satia reply that feelings have no place in an investigation.

"You're right, of course" the inspector clarifies, "but I wasn't asking whether you have any personal interests or emotional ties to the people under investigation. I was trying to gauge how you're feeling about... you know, about partnering with Kempinski and all."

"We like Kempinski!" Satia reply, "And just to be clear, Pol, nobody forced us to be on this case. We volunteered to be on it. Azucena resisted our initial request, and we had to insist. We wanted to be part of it."

> *<8C-SU BAKOLA>: We have a match; there is indeed a video of Kempinski at the SELENIC offices. The recording was made on the afternoon of July 29, the same day as the station party at New Era.*

"You like Kempinski?" Asciak slackens his walking pace so much that the Special Unit have to slow down and turn their body around to continue the conversation. "Satia, I guess it's time to recalibrate those olfactory sensors!"

> *<ELEVII'S LUNA>: Please download the video to the case repository. We need to watch it.*

Satia snicker. "Oh, come on," they add with an amused tone, "Stan is funny, and he's very good at his job. We... we like the way he looks at things."

"Do you also like the way he looks at Special Units?"

"Huh?"

"I just find it hard to understand how you can feel comfortable working with someone who thinks Special Units are not people. At least not fully. Not to mention that, for him, the fact that you are unable to break the law makes you lesser partners."

Satia keep looking at him and say nothing.

"You know what?" they say after a long pause, "I think Kempinski is right."

Baffled, Inspector Asciak suddenly stops walking.

The Special Unit also halt, seemingly taking their time to articulate their thoughts. "We mean, the Field Deputy has a point," they say with emphatic hand gestures visible to their front cameras. "How we behave is mediated by an artificial intelligence. One that monitors our biological functions and questions our intentions thousands of times every second. This is a mind that is convinced that all we ever need to be is a reliable and law-abiding security officer."

Asciak stares at Satia in disbelief. Eventually, he manages to stutter something along the lines of Special Units certainly being more than that and noting that possessing memories of their past lives must certainly count for something.

"Sure it counts for something," Satia reply, tapping a metal finger against the part of their shell that holds their organic components. "Moana Satia's memories, interests, training... most of it is still in here. When we think of ourselves, we do regard ourselves as a person. And yet, we feel that when we do that, it is simply for the sake of convenience. We cannot speak for all Special Units, but our calling ourselves a 'person' comes out of habit, not conviction. It's like—like using the same name for two different things."

> *<8C-SU BAKOLA>: Done. We have isolated the parts of the video feed that feature Kempinski. It is in our database, ready to watch.*
>
> *<ELEVII'S LUNA>: Thank you.*
>
> *<ELEVII'S LUNA>: Any guesses as to why he's lying to us?*

"We do not age like you, Pol. Nor do we feel pain. And we understand the reasons for that; allowing us to suffer physically would be inconvenient for all parties involved. Sadistic, even. But, without pain and without the possibility to freely decide how to act... we mean, how much can you take away from a person and still call them a person?"

<Pol Asciak>: Can we take a break? Or better yet, can we just stop this entirely?

<Elevii A. Tarkka ★☆☆>: [Pauses the video] Do you find this uncomfortable?

<Pol Asciak>: I don't find it uncomfortable; I find it to be a waste of time! This stuff is inconsequential for the Vannevar case. What are we doing here?

<Elevii A. Tarkka ★☆☆>: Irrelevant as they might seem, these conversations allow me to form a clearer idea of what you thought of Kempinski and how you acted in the context of the investigative team. And let me also add, Mister Asciak, that it is your legal right to refuse to answer or to withhold additional contextual information, but you are in no position to criticize my process. Do you understand?

<Pol Asciak>: I do.
[Pauses] Then I have no comment concerning the very useful conversation we have just seen. Can we move on now? [Leans back in his chair, crossing his arms]

<8C-SU BAKOLA>: We presume he is lying for the same reason he is resisting your general line of inquiry.

I resumed playing the video to see the conclusion of the conversation between Satia and Asciak. Satia raise the point that, legally speaking, Special Units are also owned by the security station where they work. They are property. If one believes Special Units should be recognized as people, they assert, it follows logically that one should also be prepared to classify them as slaves. In the interrogation room, Mister Asciak remained stubbornly silent as the video continued to play.

<ELEVII'S LUNA>: Elaborate please.

> <8C-SU BAKOLA>: *Simply put, we believe Asciak wants to avoid being portrayed as having an antagonistic, mistrustful attitude toward Kempinski.*

After we finished watching the footage, I proposed that we stop for the day. Everyone agreed immediately. With the intercession of Merel Asciak, we arranged to resume the deposition in the morning on August 28, ~~that is in two days' time, as tomorrow is a Day of Rest for most of the station's staff.~~

<NOTE> The part that follows is not relevant to the investigation and should be removed from the report before submission. It covers a conversation I had with Bakola after the Asciaks had left the room. I am leaving it here for now for personal reference.
</NOTE>

File ID: KC04
N.E. 330 – August 26, 16:41
[8C-SU Bakola (6584AR-4)]
(text automatically generated from video)

<Self ☆>: Good work today, Captain!

<Elevii A. Tarkka ★☆☆>: I feel the same way. Well done, team!

<Self ☆>: Sorry if our messages distracted you during the deposition.

<Elevii A. Tarkka ★☆☆>: Oh, not at all! I liked being able to share information and ideas in real time. Very handy. No pun intended.

<Self ☆>: [We chortle]

<Elevii A. Tarkka ★☆☆>: Also, thanks for saving the SELENIC video to our repository. That will give me something to do tomorrow. [Smiles]

<Self ☆>: Is that really how you are intending to spend the Day of Rest? Do you have no friends in this sector to visit? [Tilting our body slightly to the left]

<Elevii A. Tarkka ★☆☆>: Pathetic, I know.

<NOTE> At this point in our exchange, I was tempted to ask them what *their* plans were. I was curious to find out more about what Special Units do when they are not at work. Now that I think about it, neither Bakola nor Satia were anywhere to be seen at the New Era security party. I read somewhere that most of them spend their time off work plugged into massive online multiplayer videogame worlds. In those worlds, the article reported, Special Units are free to behave however they desire—well, within the boundaries of the game's designed affordances and possibilities. In any case, afraid to sound indelicate, I decided to drop the topic entirely. </NOTE>

<Elevii A. Tarkka ★☆☆>: Before you go, do you mind if I ask you something about today's deposition?

<Self ☆>: Of course we don't mind. It's literally part of our job.

<Elevii A. Tarkka ★☆☆>: Okay, but please be aware that this may be only tangentially related to the case, and it might make you uncomfortable. What I'm trying to say is that you absolutely don't need to answer this if you don't want to...

<Self ☆>: We think we know where this is going, Captain. This is about what Satia said, right?

<Elevii A. Tarkka ★☆☆>: It is. [Pauses] I... I was wondering if the frustration and derealization that Satia described in the corridor extract resonates with your own experience. I mean, are those feelings common among Special Units?

<Self ☆>: They are, in a sense, yes. And yet, in another sense, they are not.

<Elevii A. Tarkka ★☆☆>: Hmm?

<Self ☆>: That our training and passion for security work did not go to waste following our first death is of course something that most of us cherish. Some Special Units, however, deal with their loss better than others. And Satia...

> [We hesitate] You see, Moana Satia was a young woman when she died. We therefore think it is normal for Satia to experience a heightened sense of disconnection and frustration. We all do, in some way, at times.
>
> <Elevii A. Tarkka ★☆☆>: Including yourself?

<NOTE> I remember thinking, at this point, about how Autumn Bakola had a wife when she died. </NOTE>

> <Self ☆>: We do, indeed, but we find that it helps to keep a more pragmatic attitude.
> [We chortle] As we see it, being a Special Unit beats being dead any day of the week!
>
> <Elevii A. Tarkka ★☆☆>: Now that's a positive spin. [Smiles]
>
> <Self ☆>: Speaking of a positive spin, here is a joke for you. Do you know what is the biggest difference between being human and being a crab?
>
> <Elevii A. Tarkka ★☆☆>: No?
>
> <Self ☆>: It's—
> [We pause] It's how they have a blast!
> [We laugh]

I did not immediately understand that the punchline was a reference to something that was brought up today in the deposition, namely Special Units' capability of blowing themselves up in self-defense. I chuckled out of courtesy anyway. I am beginning to think that perhaps Kempinski was right about the cyborgs' sense of humor after all.

DAY OF REST

August 27 – Hotel Babylon 8C

<NOTE> What follows is an account of what I did on my first Day of Rest since my temporary transfer to Station 8C. I am uncertain regarding how much of this material will be relevant to the case and therefore decided to keep everything, unedited, for now for my own personal reference. I have also identified several potentially useful personal log entries from that day and added them to this file in case any part of these accounts should turn out to be relevant to the investigation, and as such worth including in the final edit of my report. If any sections should be retained, I will need to make sure to keep only what is relevant and remove the rest of that text from the final edit. </NOTE>

**** Personal Log, 8/27/330 ****

I'll start with a confession: I have always found it hard to switch from one task to another, especially when the activities concerned are both cognitively demanding. To put it simply, I quickly become stressed when handling more than one or two tasks of this nature in the same workday. To ensure that I can concentrate on one activity per day, to the extent that this is possible, I tend to plan my schedule weeks in advance. Preparation and scheduling are key in dealing with this single-track brain of mine. Relatedly, I know myself well enough not to expect to be able to turn my "work mode" off from one day to the next. My serial, task-related inertia is actually so bad that, upon waking up today, I seriously considered going to the station to work. I could easily picture myself spending the Day of Rest in those quasi-deserted offices, devoting my time to taking care of administrative chores. I'm not embarrassed to admit how desirable this prospect actually sounded to me. I didn't go to the station, though. Instead, I tried to plan a different kind of day for myself. A day that I decided to start by allowing myself to enjoy the comfort of my bed longer than usual. The enjoyment I derived from lying there awake, from simply existing in the warm embrace of the comforter, lasted a few inconsequential minutes. Thoughts about the case soon started to surface in my conscious mind. The first of these was of Pol Asciak and his abrupt confession. Was his admission of guilt just a foolish attempt from the investigator to regain some control over his own life? Then, I thought of Bakola and suddenly realized that the Special Unit assisting me on this case had access to the staff's query logs on the station's mainframe. Just yesterday afternoon, they had reconstructed some of Asciak's activities by analyzing entries in his search history, meaning that Bakola had—at the very least—the same level of clearance I did. Had the Special Unit also examined my query log? And, if so, had Bakola noticed that I looked up information about them, the circumstances of their death, and the whereabouts of their former wife? I pushed my face hard against the pillow, hoping to make the jittery feeling I had go away. After this proved unsuccessful, I got up and tried to find respite from restless thoughts by using half of my daily water allowance to take a shower.

The restaurant of the hotel where I'm staying has actual windows and is located just a few floors below my single-occupancy room. I'm grateful to the staff of Station 8C for arranging these accommodations. This morning, instead of distractedly grabbing a nutrient bar from the hotel lobby on my way to the station, I decided to treat myself to a proper breakfast, enhanced by an actual view of the outside world, with abundant hydroponic beans and strips of bacon fresh from the geno-sequencers. In a supplementary attempt to give the day a trajectory that differed from my usual routine, I brought the copy of *Antigone* with me. I intended to start reading the book I had received from the major during my morning meal. Little did I know that *Antigone* is not your regular novel. It is indeed a work of fiction, but it has the ungainly form of a drama script: the text for a play (now supposedly even more appealing thanks to a foreword written by a contemporary literary figure I had never heard of). As someone who hardly ever engages in reading for pleasure, I found that the book's format made it extra difficult for me to appreciate its content, not to mention that every time a character opened their mouth, it was to deliver a haughty and insufferable public speech of some sort.

About 20 other hotel guests were enjoying their morning meal with me next to the same large south-facing window overlooking the Antarctic plains. It didn't take long for ideas about the case to begin to push their way back into my mind, sending any thoughts of the old city of Thebes and its ruler scuttling away like frightened mice. My desire to have a special morning proved impossible to fulfill. It was an uphill struggle to begin with, as I had already been focused exclusively on my new case for several days. Deputy Bakola would probably associate these behavioral urges with my fear of failure, and they wouldn't be wrong about that. I took a long, deep breath and forced myself to remain sitting by the window for an additional minute or two.

Back in my room, I activated my LUNA's network connection. An alert welcomed me as soon as I logged in: a new message from Major Azucena. Her carefully worded squeak was an attempt to schedule a one-to-one meeting with me, with her earliest availability for this being late in the afternoon tomorrow. In light of what I had found out about Vannevar's profile, I had honestly expected her to reach out to me earlier, and with more urgency. I shouldn't worry about this, though. It's her job, I thought, and this is her station. In any case, I knew better than to put additional pressure on my host-chief.

The meeting she proposed would also be an opportunity to update her on how Pol Asciak's deposition was going. Judging from the wording of Azucena's message, she seemed to think that we would also have time for a more personal kind of exchange. I got the idea that she meant to check on my satisfaction with the work environment and ask whether I felt I was receiving enough support with the investigation, which was fair enough.

I quickly livenoted a positive response to Azucena's squeak-message.

After thanking her for setting up the meeting, I confirmed my availability to meet the next day. After that, I navigated the mainframe database to the repository for my current case, a digital space I shared with Deputy Bakola. The most recently added among a growing number of case files was the video the Special Unit had extracted and saved during yesterday's deposition: Field Deputy Kempinski's visit to the administrative offices of SELENIC on the afternoon of July 29. With a few gestures of my LUNA, I selected and launched the file. Immediately, my visor split into four rectangular sub-screens. Each of the four sectors I was looking at corresponded to a different point of view on the same scene, synchronously monitoring both the inside and the outside of SELENIC's small and unremarkable center of operations in this sector.

Had Clem Young followed the same tower-wide security prescriptions as SELENIC, he would have saved Station 8C a lot of trouble, not to mention staff hours, computational power, and the cost of my own transport, inter-sector checks, and hotel room, and the list goes on...

****

The upper left portion of the video looks down on a dimly lit backstreet. This feed was shot from a point of view positioned above the entrance to the administrative offices. From here, a bright and bustling street is visible at the far end of the alley. A white electric vehicle is parked immediately below the camera recording this scene. This vehicle has the blue tripartite SELENIC logo printed on its sides and on its roof.

<NOTE> I briefly paused the video here and used my terminal to identify the larger pathway intersecting the SELENIC backstreet as the Bonnelle Ring, which is a popular commercial avenue that links several of the sector's recreational hubs. The New Era Diner

and Café (the location where Asciak and Kempinski first talked about the case) is on another offshoot of the same avenue, just three blocks away from the SELENIC offices. </NOTE>

The slice of the Bonnelle Ring captured by this security camera is alive with vehicular traffic. Notwithstanding the distance, I could also make out a steady flow of pedestrians, as well as the occasional service automaton sidling around. The vitality of one of the biggest arteries of the sector does not, however, bleed into the small alley primarily monitored by SELENIC's first security camera; this area remains dark and lifeless for the first few minutes of the footage.

The second quadrant of the video—the one occupying the upper right portion of my visor—corresponds to a wide-angle camera hanging from the ceiling of the administrative offices' back room. The pea-green postplastic floor of this rather large space is spotted with old grease stains. Against one of the walls stands a bulky terminal, flanked on either side by recharging stations of the kind used for transport automata and small electric vehicles. A closed rolling shutter occupies most of the opposite wall. My guess was that this opens to the aforementioned alley monitored by the external security camera, but I could not verify my assumption from the video feed, as the shutter remains closed for the duration of the recording. Two white T1 platform automata with SELENIC logos printed on their sides blink rhythmically in the center of the room, as if they have dozed off while waiting for their next call.

The bottom two sectors of the four-part view offer complementary views of the front office. The bottom left quadrant looks over the reception counter, whereas the bottom right one monitors the entrance area. The latter consists of an open door and an empty bench that, as far as I could tell, is the same model as the one outside the elevator in Room B0 at the station. A portion of a door to a small bathroom is also visible, not far from the bench.

Behind the reception counter, in the bottom left quadrant of my screen, a young person is sucking on a lollipop while killing time by playing a garish videogame. Their gender and genetic heritage are difficult to determine from the recording. The interface overlay identifies the androgynous clerk as male—a Sector 8C resident by the name of Josiah Dechpang. Dechpang appears to have no history of security infractions. Another thing Josiah does not seem to have is anything urgent to do: he spends the first few minutes of the video playing his videogame on one of the two terminal screens in front of him. Not far from the screens is a small and colorful shrine, a "spirit house" of sorts. The shrine features a votive vase full of sand. Planted in the sand are three thin candles, two of which are lit.

Again, for the first few minutes of the video, nothing of note happens either outside or inside the SELENIC administrative offices. Josiah changes the position of the lollipop in his mouth a few times, the screen of the videogame flashes with bright colors every now and then, and the two platform automata remain sound asleep in the back office. The lack of activity makes me wonder if Deputy Bakola had extracted the right footage recorded at SELENIC that day. The hustling and bustling at the end of the alley also continues unremarkably.

About two minutes into the video, a dark silhouette ambles unsteadily into the SELENIC alley from the brightly lit background of the Bonnelle Ring. As it advances towards the administrative offices, it becomes clear that the figure is a 'he'. He has made it about halfway down the alley when the automatic streetlights suddenly turn on, allowing the facial recognition software to recognize Field Deputy Stan Kempinski's features. The new lighting conditions in the alley also reveal some words that had been hastily painted on the peeling plaster of one of the walls. It looks like they say

"LET'S MAKE BRICKS

AND BAKE THEM THOROUGHLY."

But I am not entirely sure, as the distance and the camera angle make these words rather difficult to read.

Kempinski walks unsteadily in the direction of the office entrance. Having nearly reached his destination, he leans against one of the alley walls and—partly covered by the parked electric vehicle—unzips his pants. His left hand rests against the wall to keep him steady while his right hand... well, let's say "directs operations." While relieving himself, the field deputy looks around the alley as if searching for something or possibly making a belated attempt to ensure that he is indeed alone. When he is done, he zips his fly back up and rubs his hands on his coat. I can picture Pol Asciak's face as he watched this portion of the footage, shivering with disgust at the idea that he had shaken that very hand at the office party later the same day.

Kempinski climbs the three concrete steps to the SELENIC administrative offices, nearly missing the first one. In the bottom right quadrant of the screen, I see him entering the office and heading toward the counter where Josiah is still playing his game.

The field deputy then stands beside the reception counter, where he is blatantly ignored by the clerk.

"You winnin', bub?" he asks, half a minute later.

> File ID: KC09
> N.E. 330 – July 29, 17:21
> [SELENIC 8C (R3)]
> (text automatically generated from video)
>
> <Josiah Dechpang>: [Unintelligible mumbling]
>
> <Stanisław Kempinski ☆☆>: I'm sorry, what's that?
>
> <Josiah Dechpang>: [Takes the lollipop out of his mouth] [Turns toward Kempinski] I said that this is just a pastime. Winning isn't the point.
>
> <Stanisław Kempinski ☆☆>: Ah! That's what I always say about games: it doesn't really matter if you win; what matters is whether Kempinski wins.
>
> <Josiah Dechpang>: [Appearing confused] Kempinski?
>
> <Stanisław Kempinski ☆☆>: That would be me. [Showing his security wrist badge] Station 8C.
>
> <Josiah Dechpang>: [Pauses the game] Well, it's a pleasure to make your acquaintance, Officer Kempinski. How can SELENIC help you today?
>
> <Stanisław Kempinski ☆☆>: Are you the manager here?

<Josiah Dechpang>: Assistant Manager, sir. At your service.

<Stanisław Kempinski ☆☆>: Your services might be just what I need. You see, I'm looking for information. A name. Just let me—

At that point, Kempinski starts rummaging through the pockets of his trousers. His laborious search produces, in this order, a used napkin, a candy wrapper, a set of keys, and finally a crumpled, yellowish paper note. The field deputy puts the keys back in his pocket and slides the paper note across the reception counter to Josiah, leaving the rest of his treasures splayed out on the counter.

<Stanisław Kempinski ☆☆>: Here are some ride details. I need the name of the person who was in this vehicle.

<Josiah Dechpang>: [Picks up the note]

<Stanisław Kempinski ☆☆>: And the name of whoever paid for it. You know, in case they are different people. Please and thank you.

<Josiah Dechpang>: [Reads the text on the note] I'd sure love to help, Deputy. But you know as well as I do that I cannot disclose that information. Not without an official warrant, I mean. As you might remember from our advertisements, our company goes the extra mile to protect the privacy of its patrons and customers.

<Stanisław Kempinski ☆☆>: But of course!

<Josiah Dechpang>: Excellent! Come back with a warrant, and my colleagues and I will be more than happy to share the information with you.
[Slides the note back to Kempinski]

<Stanisław Kempinski ☆☆>: Right.
[Pauses] I *could* do that. Or...
[Scratching his chin] Or you could spare me the pain. You see, going back to ask the chief for authorization, then going to the station's legal office to wait for my warrant, and finally coming back here again to see you lovely people... well, it's going to be a drag. Why don't we just skip to the part where you print the information I need so we both can get on with our days?

<NOTE> This was a half-truth at best. When Kempinski visited SELENIC, the Vannevar case had not yet been officially launched. Obtaining a warrant without an ongoing investigation wouldn't be as easy as he made it sound. </NOTE>

<Josiah Dechpang>: Afraid not, Officer. My boss would not appreciate that, and I would get in a lot of trouble if she found out. Here at SELENIC, we play by the rules, if you know what I mean.

<Stanisław Kempinski ☆☆>: I think I know what you mean, yes.
[Puts his hands back in his pockets] So this is like a game, huh?

<Josiah Dechpang>: [Appearing confused] That... that's not what I—

<Stanisław Kempinski ☆☆>: [Interrupting] Okay, then. Let's play.

Kempinski smiles and slowly turns around. Then he casually strolls out of the office door, climbs down the entrance steps, and walks farther up the alley. He eventually moves beyond the frame of the upper left quadrant of the video. When he walks back, ten to fifteen seconds later, Kempinski is holding a thick postplastic pipe, dripping with what appears to be water. When he sees the officer back into the administrative office holding the pipe, Josiah lets the lollipop drop from his mouth. Obviously alarmed, the assistant manager tries to de-escalate the situation.

<Josiah Dechpang>: Officer, please. You... we are being recorded.
[Points in the direction of the two security cameras in the front office] I don't—

<Stanisław Kempinski ☆☆>: Oh, this?!
[Raises the pipe]
[Cackles] There seems to be a misunderstanding, bub. I'm not planning on using this on you!
[Smiles] ...Also not on your videogame. Don't worry.

<NOTE> At this point, Kempinski is standing right in front of the

counter, holding the pipe. </NOTE>

<Josiah Dechpang>: Sir, can—
[Takes a step back]

<Stanisław Kempinski ☆☆>: [Interrupting] But I regret to inform you that your company's recycling system hasn't been properly maintained.
[Lays the pipe on the counter] You have a broken duct. A little wasted water. Unfortunate, I would say, but not that big of a deal.

<NOTE> The pipe kept dripping, and the counter got visibly wet. Josiah stood still, frozen in place in a way that reminded me of an automaton asked to perform two conflicting tasks at the same time. </NOTE>

<Stanisław Kempinski ☆☆>: Still, I'm afraid I'll have to report this infraction. You see, we both have to play by the rules.

<8C-SU BAKOLA>: Pardon the intrusion, Captain. We have received a notification of depository access through your assigned terminal and wanted to check that everything is in order, given that this is not a work day. Do you recognize this access?

<Josiah Dechpang>: I... you...

<Stanisław Kempinski ☆☆>: Okay, let me make it easier for you, bub. You have two choices. Option one: you provide me with the information I need. Option two: you insist on seeing an official warrant.
[Pauses] Pick the first, and I'll be out of your hair. Pick the second, and I'll be back tomorrow with a warrant and a fine for this infraction. I guess your boss won't appreciate that either, will she?

<ELEVII'S LUNA>: Good morning! I was just watching Kempinski's stunt at SELENIC. Thank you again for finding that.

<8C-SU BAKOLA>: Oh, so you were serious. This really is how you are spending the holiday.

The gradual thawing of Josiah's body begins with a small motion, just a twitch of the hand. The same hand then picks up the now damp paper note from Kempinski. The other hand moves, too, at first slowly, over the control panel. Eventually, both hands move together, typing. Kempinski looks around the office, seemingly bored. The Assistant Manager's hands input one last command, and a small printer under the counter starts moaning. The fruit of its labor is a single sheet of paper that Josiah finally hands to Kempinski.

> <Josiah Dechpang>: It... it happens to be only one name, sir.

Kempinski folds the sheet of paper without looking at the text on it and puts it into the patch pocket on his shirt. He smiles. "Good game," he says with a nod. Then he turns around, raises a hand to signal a goodbye, and moseys out of the office, this time for good. Behind the counter, Josiah stands still with his lips pursed, staring at the pool of water the field deputy has left behind.

> *<ELEVII'S LUNA>: Just finished. Quite a show, huh?*
>
> *<8C-SU BAKOLA>: Not what we would call outstanding police work, but we must admit that it was fun to watch. So, are you planning to process work-related footage all afternoon?*
>
> *<ELEVII'S LUNA>: Unless you have a better plan, that was the idea, yeah. I also wanted to re-watch the footage from the visit to Choksi in the detention center.*
>
> *<8C-SU BAKOLA>: Okay, we see. Yes, we do have a better plan, Captain. How about us offering to give you, as an out-of-towner, a guided tour of the neighborhood instead? You know, to get you oriented.*
>
> *<ELEVII'S LUNA>: That's a very kind offer. Are you sure you wouldn't mind?*
>
> *<8C-SU BAKOLA>: Yes, of course. We aim to be helpful!*
> *<ELEVII'S LUNA>: That's very nice of you. I accept the offer.*

> *<8C-SU BAKOLA>: One thing needs to be clear, though. This invitation is strictly informal. We are to be two colleagues hanging out in our spare time.*
> *If you are hoping that your tour will include a visit to Clem's Bar or the alley where SELENIC is located, you will be disappointed.*

**** Personal Log, 8/27/330 (cont'd) ****

I was grateful for Bakola's offer, but I was indeed about to propose visiting locations that were relevant to our investigation, including the two they gave as off-limits examples. I didn't regret accepting their offer to show me around, however. Spending the day with Bakola was a lot of fun, and—unlike my solo attempts—it did manage to effectively distract me from the case. We spent a few hours together. During that time, to my relief, Bakola didn't once mention their former wife.

****

INVESTIGATION DAY 5 (MORNING)

August 28 – SS8C

The sky outside the wall-sized window in Room B2 was still dark when I arrived on the morning of the fifth day of the investigation. ~~I sat at the table and quickly downed one of the nutrient bars I had grabbed earlier at the hotel, bracing for what I expected to be a very long day of work.~~ Sitting alone, I revised my notes, read a few sections of the report Asciak had written on the Choksi case, and sent a squeak to Bakola to let them know I was already at the station. The Special Unit and I had agreed to have a quick preparation meeting for today's deposition before the Asciaks arrived.

<NOTE> In my message, I also thanked them again for making time for me on the previous afternoon. </NOTE>

~~When the sun started to rise, partly eclipsed by the central thermosyphon, I got up from my chair and walked to the window, careful not to touch the glass. There seemed to be fewer swallows flying around today. I stood there, lost in thought; I am not sure for how long. When I roused from my daydream, the sky outside had~~

~~transitioned from purple to orange. It then turned rather quickly to the kind of milky yellow that is usually seen at the start of hot and clear winter days. It was the unexpected hiss of the elevator doors opening onto Floor B that brought me back to the present moment.~~ I had left the door to the interview room open, expecting the Special Unit to arrive. However, instead of ~~the low, angular body of~~ Deputy Bakola, I was surprised to see Captain Kutta standing in the doorway.

With a smile, he wished me a good morning. He added that he had come to the office earlier than usual, hoping to catch me alone, which was a ~~rather creepy~~ way of saying that he wanted to talk to me privately. I emphatically looked at the two cameras mounted on the ceiling of Room B2 and commented that one is never truly alone in our surveilled world.

<NOTE> A corollary of that observation is that we are never truly ourselves, either. I am referring to the fact that we are always subject to scrutiny and observation, at least potentially. Much like what occurs with the Special Units, this situation forces us into a state of constant self-regulation and self-censorship. I guess most people consider this a fair price to pay for our collective safety. </NOTE>

I walked out to stand beside Captain Kutta in the waiting area (B0) ~~and closed the door to the interview room behind me so that whatever it was that Uncle Rahman had to say would not be captured by the interrogation room's cameras or microphones.~~ The old captain smiled, and I smiled back. With a gesture, I invited him to take a seat on the bench and then sat down beside him, with the bolted table in between us.

"Do you want to tell me something that will brighten my day, Uncle Rahman?" I asked.

"I am not sure this is going to brighten anything, Elevii," he replied in a hushed tone, "but I think it is something you should know. Maybe it is nothing. And please do not livetype this, or whatever it is called. Just listen, okay?"

"Okay?" I replied, still livenoting.

"I saw Merel Asciak meeting with Major Azucena. In the chief's office. That was two days ago, quite late in the afternoon. I presume after one of your interrogation sessions."

Captain Kutta then recounted the story of how he happened to see them there—an epic narrative whose arc had its point of origin in the very room where we were sitting, with what the captain described as a "bathroom emergency." ~~Needless to say, I did not need or want to hear most of what he wanted to share, as he described his actions like those of an unassuming hero who unexpectedly found himself on a mythical quest.~~ Because of the lack of toilets on this floor, Uncle Rahman had to call the elevator and embark in a journey into peculiar kind of underworld, one that is technically located above us. Through what he described as a "veritable display of superhuman willpower," our hero survived the first leg of his expedition and reached a bathroom on the station's main floor (Floor A). And then, a tragic turn of events: on the bathroom door, he saw a large magnetic sign announcing "MAINTENANCE AND SANITATION." Shocked and now in pain, the old captain tried to push the door open anyway, but the lock would not budge. That was it: he thought he was done for, that it had all been futile. Even worse than futile, actually, as he would very soon soil himself in front of a dozen colleagues, when he could have done that in the privacy of his office. Drenched in cold sweat, he did the only thing he could do at that point: he walked on

.<NOTE> I am omitting a long part of the story both because I stopped paying attention at some point and because of its clear irrelevance to the investigation. </NOTE>

Against all odds, Uncle Rahman made it to another bathroom. He was not far from his intended destination when he saw the security chief welcoming Asciak's younger sister into her office. I found that part of his story particularly perplexing, and he must have, too. Captain Kutta's might not shine for his social acumen, but he was sensible enough to come and tell me what he saw.

<NOTE> One could argue, of course, that he relayed this information to me precisely because of, rather than in spite of, his social clumsiness. </NOTE>

I could not think of any reason why he would lie to me about this. Although it was not illegal, what Uncle Rahman had witnessed was certainly unusual: it is in fact a rather exceptional circumstance for an interviewee in a security investigation (or their legal representative for that matter) to meet privately with the upper-level police administrator who is ultimately responsible for their case.

Captain Kutta continued with his quasi-mythical tale, which climaxed—as one would expect—on the toilet. The details of his story had no bearing on my case, nor did Pol Asciak's absence from Rahman's recount. At the time, in fact, Pol Asciak was not allowed on security grounds. Following protocol, he had to be escorted off the premises at the end of each deposition session.

Partway through his vibrant description of the joy he felt as his quest was reaching its triumphant ending, Captain Kutta was interrupted by the hiss of the elevator doors opening. Emerging from the elevator this time was the six-legged mechanical body of Special Unit Deputy Bakola.

File ID: KC05
N.E. 330 – August 28, 07:52
[8C-SU Bakola (6584AR-4)]
(text automatically generated from video)

<Rahman Kutta ★☆☆>: Top of the morning, Deputy! How are we doing today?

<Self ☆>: Oh, you know, it is the beginning of a new work week. We guess it is normal if we feel a little... *crabby*! [We chuckle]

<Rahman Kutta ★☆☆>: [Laughs] Oh, you!

<Self ☆>: But seriously, are we interrupting something? We could come back in ten min—

<Rahman Kutta ★☆☆>: [Interrupting] No need, my dear. I just popped by to say hello.
[Getting up from his seat]
[Turning to Tarkka] Well, good luck today, Captain!

<Elevii A. Tarkka ★☆☆>: [Inaudible]

<Self ☆>: Knock, knock!

<Elevii A. Tarkka ★☆☆>: [Appearing confused] The door is open, Deputy, and you know you can go inside the interview room whenever you want.

<Rahman Kutta ★☆☆>: [Speaking to Tarkka] Oh, Elevii, just play along! Here, let me show you.
[Speaking to Us] Please knock again, Deputy.

<Self ☆>: [Buzzing] Knock, knock!

<Rahman Kutta ★☆☆>: [Speaking to Us] Yes...? Who's there?

<Self ☆>: [Giddy] It's Justin!

<Rahman Kutta ★☆☆>: Justin?! Justin who?

<Self ☆>: Justin time for one of your jokes!

<Rahman Kutta ★☆☆>: [Guffaws]

<Elevii A. Tarkka ★☆☆>: [Rolls her eyes]

<Self ☆>: Just a small one before you leave, Uncle Rahman. Please?

<Rahman Kutta ★☆☆>: [Scratching his chin] Hmm, a joke, huh?

<Self ☆>: Come on!

<Rahman Kutta ★☆☆>: Hmm, okay. I think I've got one for you.
[Pauses] What do you call a security department that is full of Special Units?

<Self ☆>: [We pause] A... a great work environment?

<Rahman Kutta ★☆☆>: A *crust-station*.
[Snickers] Get it?! A *crustacean*!

<Self ☆>: [We laugh uncontrollably]

~~Bakola were in hysterics for a full minute after Captain Kutta left the room. Their legs were even twitching. Eventually, once they had managed to get themselves under control, the Special Unit followed me back into the interview room and closed the door behind them.~~

Moments later, during our preliminary meeting, I briefed Bakola on the events in the Vannevar case that I intended to cover in the day's deposition and on the recorded material that I planned to use to direct the session's focus. I also informed them of my aspiration to finish Asciak's deposition by tomorrow, although I was well aware that reaching that objective depended on a number of factors, including Asciak's mood. Finally, I told Bakola about the meeting planned with Azucena in the late afternoon that day (a meeting that they—no doubt—had already spotted in our shared calendar). ~~I could not fathom any reason why they should not also attend that meeting, and so~~ I asked them if they were interested in joining. The Special Unit responded positively, at least in principle. It would ultimately be the station chief's decision, they correctly remarked.

<NOTE> I probably should remove all the text on Day 5 above this note in the final draft of my report. Maybe add a quick introduction—nothing too detailed. </NOTE>

It was almost time to invite the Asciaks into the room to begin the day's session. Before that, however, I wanted to make sure I understood something that I had forgotten to look up over the weekend. It was something that Hematsu Choksi had said in one of the videos we would review during the morning's deposition. I am including the transcript of this part of my conversation with Bakola here.

File ID: KC05
N.E. 330 – August 28, 08:48
[8C-SU Bakola (6584AR-4)]
(text automatically generated from video)

<Elevii A. Tarkka ★☆☆>: It's about what Choksi says to Asciak about halfway through the interrogation. You know, when they use the word "player."

<Self ☆>: Yes, what about it?

<Elevii A. Tarkka ★☆☆>: Can you help me understand what "player" means in this context? What makes it different from a Special Unit like yourself, for example?

<Self ☆>: Well... simply put, a "player" is a cyborg who plays in ranked *Duplicate Conduit* tournaments.

<Elevii A. Tarkka ★☆☆>: And that's it?

<Self ☆>: In short, yes.

<Elevii A. Tarkka ★☆☆>: But how does it work? I struggle to see how a cyborg could be fair competition for a human player. I mean, wouldn't that be two brains against one?

<Self ☆>: Well, that... that is a harder question. [We pause] How much time do we have?

<Elevii A. Tarkka ★☆☆>: [Checks the palm of her LUNA] Not much, but I would be very grateful if you tried.

<Self ☆>: Okay. As you suggest, a cyborg's artificial intelligence is not simply an interface between a human brain and a mechanical body. It is a mind of its own... and a significantly autonomous one at that. For instance, it handles many of the brain functions that were originally handled by the biological resident's limbic system.

<NOTE> I was not surprised to learn that the limbic system is also one of the key systems involved in understanding and appreciating humor. </NOTE>

<Elevii A. Tarkka ★☆☆>: [Nods] Please continue.

<Self ☆>: The work done by the T3 intelligence in the background is what allows the cyborg not to need to learn how to operate its new body from scratch, like a newborn does. And that is not all. Under the hood, the shell's artificial intelligence also handles autonomic processes like regulating the temperature of the brain and monitoring the chemical composition and acidity of the cerebrospinal fluid.

<Elevii A. Tarkka ★☆☆>: A cyborg's artificial intelligence is also autonomously responsible for some of your high-level

behaviors, right? I know it's mandatory that the code of law is embedded in the T3 software of every shell.

<Self ☆>: As a measure to prevent deviant or criminal behavior, yes, which makes a lot of sense, considering how dangerous cyborgs are, potentially. But we are getting sidetracked.
[Tilting our body upward] Now, I am not an expert here, but I know that *Duplicate Conduit* is a game that relies on lateral thinking, the figurative use of language, and the subtle manipulation of other players. Our T3 struggles with interactions at that level of ambiguity and social embeddedness. So much so, in fact, that competing in *Duplicate Conduit* as a cyborg player is typically considered a handicap rather than a performative advantage.

<NOTE> Here, Bakola referred to the fact that the organic brains of cyborg players often need to make strategic decisions in relation to their opponents while also maneuvering around the artificial intelligence with which they are coupled. </NOTE>

<Elevii A. Tarkka ★☆☆>: So you're telling me that there are no structural differences between a cyborg player and a Special Unit?

<Self ☆>: Same setup, same everything. The only difference is that the organic bits of players are very good at *Conduit*. Oh, and also that their rebirths are typically financed by private wealth instead of being sponsored by the federal government. Special Units' rebirths are free of charge, but we are brought back from the dead to be public servants... as public property, some would say.

<Elevii A. Tarkka ★☆☆>: So, a "player" is a privately owned cyborg.

<Self ☆>: One whose *Duplicate Conduit* skills and reputation justified the price of the operation, the shell, and all the rest, yes. Privately owned cyborgs are obviously quite rare, given how expensive they are.

<NOTE> I stood up and walked around Room B2, hoping the movement would help me wrap my mind around this idea.

I wondered whether one could sponsor one's own rebirth, which would result in a cyborg being self-owned. </NOTE>

<Self ☆>: Shall we call the Asciaks in?

<Elevii A. Tarkka ★☆☆>: Just one more minute, please. [Pauses] So, what happens if a cyborg becomes disloyal to their owner? Can a player get bored with *Duplicate Conduit* and stop putting serious effort into the game? What if a player refuses to play altogether?

<Self ☆>: Keeping a cyborg motivated could be a challenge. We do not have a great deal of information about privately owned cyborgs, but we can tell you what would happen to a Special Unit in that predicament.

<Elevii A. Tarkka ★☆☆>: Do you mean in case you become apathetic and refuse to do security work?

<Self ☆>: Precisely. Should one of us exhibit that kind of behavior, they would receive a couple of official warnings. Eventually, if the attitude were to persist, the owner—a station, in this case—could take more drastic measures. We can be put into stasis for a certain amount of time, or even shut down permanently.
[We pause] At that point, we are to be decommissioned and scrapped for parts.

File ID: KC05
N.E. 330 – August 28, 10:02
[8C-SU Bakola (6584AR-4)]
(text automatically generated from video)

<Elevii A. Tarkka ★☆☆>: All right, this is the third day of Mister Asciak's deposition. As always, his testimony is meant to contribute to the evidentiary body of an internal investigation concerning the Vannevar case. The date is August the 28th, 330. It is just past 10 in the morning. Also present at the deposition is Merel Asciak in her role as Mister Asciak's legal representative.

[Speaking to Pol and Merel Asciak] Welcome back, both of you.

<Pol Asciak>: Thank you.

<Merel Asciak>: [Smiles]

<Elevii A. Tarkka ★☆☆>: [Speaking to Pol Asciak] Mister Asciak, we closed the last session with a discussion of the events that followed the first meeting of the newly formed investigative team tasked with working the Vannevar case. I am referring to the afternoon of July 30th.

<Pol Asciak>: That's right.

<Elevii A. Tarkka ★☆☆>: [Checking her notes] And at the end of that meeting, you and Field Deputy Kempinski agreed that the next logical step in your investigation would be to pay a visit to Hematsu Choksi, whom you had personally arrested a few weeks prior and who, at the time, was in custody at the local detention center, awaiting his trial.

<Pol Asciak>: We needed more information about Vannevar. Since we were after clues and new directions, we saw talking to Choksi as the lowest-hanging investigative fruit to pick, so to speak.

<NOTE> Pol Asciak seemed calmer during this third session. At least, I got the sense that he was less despondent and less suspicious of me. I assumed he had found a way to unwind during the Day of Rest and let go of some of his negative thoughts. It was only the next day that I found out the real reasons behind his transformation and the role his sister had played in bringing that change about by giving him a concrete future path, presumably arranged through her off-the-books meeting with Azucena just before the Day of Rest. </NOTE>

<Elevii A. Tarkka ★☆☆>: Noted. Could you summarize the various steps that led to you interviewing Choksi?

<Pol Asciak>: [Thinking] Sure... [Pauses] After the initial meeting in Kempinski's office, Satia and I had the chat that we watched during the last

session. I'm referring to the one in the corridor. After that... well, I went back to the chief's office to obtain the authorizations needed to interview that son of a bitch inside the detention facility.

<Merel Asciak>: [Clears her throat]

<Pol Asciak>: Yeah, pardon my language.

<Elevii A. Tarkka ★☆☆>: Please continue.

<Pol Asciak>: And I guess that pretty much sums it up. We obtained the necessary permits, and, the following morning, the three of us were on our way up to talk to Choksi. It didn't take too long to get there, although inter-sector checks seem to be taking longer and longer to process. Have you noticed that, too?

<Elevii A. Tarkka ★☆☆>: Kind of, yeah. Anyway, getting back to Choksi, did the team agree on a strategy for the interview?

<Pol Asciak>: Yes, that is practically all we talked about during the trip. After some discussion, we agreed on a one-on-one approach: Choksi was going to face me alone, while Kempinski and Satia monitored the interview from a nearby control room. The plan was to drop Vannevar's name right at the beginning of the conversation. We were going for a funk.

<Elevii A. Tarkka ★☆☆>: Please explain.

<Self>: [Tilting our body slightly to the side]

<Pol Asciak>: A funk. As in a state of elevated stress. Our goal was to induce an intense emotional state in the interviewee. Strategically, we planned to play the Vannevar card right away to provoke an impulsive reaction in Choksi.

<Elevii A. Tarkka ★☆☆>: Was sending you in particular also supposed to put additional emotional pressure on Choksi?

<Pol Asciak>: That was actually my idea, yes. It was me who raided his warehouse and brought him to that detention

facility... We assumed that having to talk to me alone would make the situation even more uncomfortable and stressful for the creep and increase the chance of mistakes, slip-ups, and the like.

<Elevii A. Tarkka ★☆☆>: Noted.
[Pauses] If it's okay, I suggest that we watch the recording of that interview.

<Pol Asciak>: No objections.
[Takes a sip of water from the glass in front of him]

With a gesture of my LUNA two-thumber, I selected and played the video that I had chosen the previous night. This particular video was downloaded from the detention center's archive.

At the beginning of the video, Asciak is alone in a white-walled fluorescent-lit room. He is wearing his full police uniform and sitting in a sturdy aluminum chair. There are two more chairs identical to this one arranged around a metal table, which is bolted to the floor. The table features a kick guard, as well as a small constellation of restraint rings. A heavy-looking door with a small, horizontal window stands ajar. The numbers "2" and "3" are stenciled directly on the door's metal surface in white paint, separated by a vertical segment, also white.

Asciak sits motionless, his arms crossed and his elbows resting atop the metal surface of the table. About a minute and a half into the video, two prison guards—both men, one with a cybernetic leg from the knee down—enter the room. They are escorting Hematsu Choksi, one on either side of the detainee, holding him. Choksi's hands are tied behind his oversized prison uniform. The guards tower over the small man, whose diminutive stature is further emphasized by the posture induced by the handcuffs. Choksi is invited to sit in one of the chairs with firmness but without the use of force. The guards secure the detainee's handcuffs to one of the table's restraint rings. Throughout the entirety of this process, Asciak sits perfectly still.

"Inspector, it is such a delight to meet you again!" Choksi exclaims garishly. "To what do I owe the honor?"

Asciak does not acknowledge Choksi's question.

The prison guards exchange a nod and split up: the man with the artificial leg remains in the interrogation room, while the other guard walks out of the room and locks the heavy door behind him. The latter will remain outside, keeping watch.

"I take it you've been missing me," Choksi teases, with the evident intent of establishing that he is in control of his emotions and will not succumb to any planned intimidation.

Asciak laughs through his nose. It is the first time he has moved in the last three minutes.

"Come on! Admitting to having feelings isn't a sign of weakness... just the opposite, in fact."

Asciak straightens up and says something to the effect of him not batting an eye if all crooks like Choksi were to just up and disappear from the face of the planet tomorrow.

"Harsh! So harsh, Inspector. But please consider what a loss that would be for the human race. Hear me out: what if... what if the same cluster of genes responsible for what you might call 'criminal behavior' is also responsible for promoting experimentation? You know, challenging the status quo and pushing against cultural boundaries and norms? What if mavericks like myself are the actual driving force behind social change?"

"Clearly you are doing God's work," Asciak comments, unamused.

"I might be! Weren't several great philosophers, poets, and artists also accused of cri—"

"That's enough, creep."

Asciak's sudden change in tone frightens the detainee and stops him dead in his tracks. It seems that he is not as impervious to manipulation as he has just tried to make himself out to be, after all.

"I am here to ask you about Egon Vannevar," the inspector says after a few seconds of silence.

"E-egon who?"

Asciak has video evidence that Choksi worked as an intermediary in an illegal inter-sector delivery involving Vannevar. The inspector calmly lets the detainee know as much. Upon hearing Asciak's description of the delivery, Choksi's posture changes visibly.

With a smile, the detainee advises the inspector to make peace with the fact that he will not be getting anything out of him and invites Asciak to skip the whole "put in a good word with the judge kind of bullshit."

On the opposite side of the metal table, Asciak's body tenses. Moments later, he draws in a deep breath and leans back in his chair. He then puts his hands behind his head, lacing his fingers together, and sighs, looking up at the ceiling. "Well, I tried."

Choksi smiles again and shakes his head. "Tried and succeeded to waste time, both yours and mine," he says."

Last I heard, you're looking at six years in the jug. That will be plenty of time to do whatever it is that you're anxious to do in your miserable, windowless hole. And I mean six years without taking into account the crab whose import you *failed to declare*."

<NOTE> Asciak set off the last few words with air quotes. His use of slur words in this interaction is uncharacteristic of him and was presumably done for show. </NOTE>

Choksi tuts at Asciak for being a tryhard. "That was pathetic, Inspector," he says, adding, with the tone of an offhand comment, "and besides, a player is not even illegal goods. What difference is it going to make to my sentence?"

A player.

Asciak tenses up again, but this time he manages to conceal his emotions well enough. "We'll see about that," he utters mechanically, although his mind is racing. "We will see," he repeats, staring directly into the eye of the camera monitoring the room.

I decided to pause the video at this climactic moment.

File ID: KC05
N.E. 330 – August 28, 09:39
[8C-SU Bakola (6584AR-4)]
(text automatically generated from video)

<Elevii A. Tarkka ★☆☆>: That was... [Shakes her head] quite impressive!

<Pol Asciak>: Yeah, I guess it was one of those moments. [Smiles] To be honest with you, that was a bit of a Hail Mary play.

<Elevii A. Tarkka ★☆☆>: If that was a lucky shot, it was a lucky shot you set up for yourselves.

<Pol Asciak>: Yeah, I guess. In a sense.

<Elevii A. Tarkka ★☆☆>: Is there anything you would like to add to what we just watched?

<Pol Asciak>: No, but there are a couple of points I'll need to clarify coming up shortly.

<Elevii A. Tarkka ★☆☆>: [Nods] Very well. Now, for this next part, we're going to take Deputy Satia's point of view.

I then played Satia's footage for that day from a timestamp I had set for this occasion. In this video extract, Satia sit in front of a screen inside one of the detention center's control rooms. On a chair next to the Special Unit, Kempinski is loudly chewing on a nutrient bar that he apparently picked up somewhere. Both he and Satia appear to be fully engrossed in what is happening on the screen in front of them.

"That was pathetic, Inspector," Choksi says in the video they are watching, "and besides, a player is not even illegal goods. What difference is it going to make to my sentence?"

"We'll see about that," Asciak replies after a short pause. "We will see," he repeats, looking straight at his colleagues at the other end of the cable.

Kempinski jolts up from his chair, unable to contain his excitement. "A player! A player, Satia! Our boy is good! Real good," he exclaims pointing at the screen with the nutrient bar.

"So the footage did not capture an uninhabited shell, after all. We see," Satia comment.

On the screen in front of them, Asciak is struggling to keep Choksi engaged. The inspector tries to bargain and ask questions, but the detainee is barely listening. He is not even looking at Asciak anymore. Choksi's body language is that of someone who has checked out of the conversation. At some point, he even addresses the prison guard in the room, asking them to escort him back to his cell.

Inside the control room, still rattling with excitement, Kempinski asks Satia if they could find out when the shell model they saw in the warehouse video had become commercially available.

"That new LUNA? Let me check..." the Special Unit perform a quick squeak search that is visible on their interface overlay. Apparently, the particular LUNA model that Vannevar collected from Choksi was brought to market just this past February. That meant that the shell in the warehouse video was, at most, four months old at the time.

"Could you also tell me how many ranked *Duplicate Conduit* players were reborn in that particular shell model in the timeframe from the start of its availability on the market to when the warehouse video was shot?"

"I certainly can."

Within a few seconds, Satia's mainframe query returns three names, listed alphabetically. They read the names aloud.

"Can... can you repeat the second name on the list?"

"Rainforest 'Rainn' Kikinda. He was a second-division player based in Byrgius, Moon."

Kempinski turns pale, and stares at Satia in disbelief.

"I... I think I need to sit for a moment," he mutters.

"Stan? Stan, are you okay?"

File ID: KC05
N.E. 330 – August 28, 09:39
[8C-SU Bakola (6584AR-4)]
(text automatically generated from video)

<Elevii A. Tarkka ★☆☆>: Had you heard that name before your visit to the detention center, Mister Asciak?

<Pol Asciak>: Rainforest Kikinda? No, that was the first time. But as I said, I was not at all familiar with *Duplicate Conduit* or its competitive scene prior to working on the Vannevar case.

<Elevii A. Tarkka ★☆☆>: Yes, you mentioned that. Was there something you wanted to add regarding the video segment we just watched?

<Pol Asciak>: This is not the part I wanted to talk about. That part is just a few minutes ahead.

<Elevii A. Tarkka ★☆☆>: I think I know exactly the part you mean.
[Gestures with her LUNA]

I picked the second timestamp in Deputy Satia's footage that I had prepared for review that day and resumed playing the video. In it, Kempinski is walking down one of the detention center's corridors, followed by the Special Unit. He seems to be feeling better, judging by the brisk resolve in his step.

The field deputy walks up to the prison guard in front of a door with a small glass window and shows him his security wrist badge. The guard unlocks the door and lets Kempinski and Satia inside. In the interrogation room, Choksi comes alive again. I presume he associated the unlocking of the door with the imminent end of his torment. His hope turns to disappointment when he sees two more security officers walk in instead. ~~Choksi's eyes briefly dart toward Satia, then back to Kempinski.~~

"Oh, please!" he whines, "It took me half an hour to get it through your boyfriend's thick skull that I'm not going to collaborate. This is getting tires—"

"Oh, I apologize, bub." Kempinski interrupts him in a higher tone of voice.

"I must have given you the impression that I came in here to listen to your crap." Stymied, Choksi raises his eyebrows.

"Now scram, the adults need to use this room." Kempinski gestures to the guard with the cybernetic leg to come and unlock Choksi to take him away.

Speechless, Asciak stares at Kempinski, uncertain as to what to do.

"Shorty's too far down the food chain to have even heard of Kikinda anyway."

"Oh, my poor heart…" the detainee retorts sarcastically.

"Just fuck off!" Kempinski barks back while the prison guard detaches Choksi from the table's restraint ring.

The detainee gets up slowly and the guard escorts him toward the door. As he walks out of the room, he smiles and says to Kempinski "You're wrong about Kikinda, pig!" Indifferent to Choksi's parting words, the field deputy pushes the heavy door shut.

"Now who or what the fuck is a Kikinda?" Asciak asks, irritated. Then he stands up and demands to know why Kempinski thought it was a good idea to barge in like that.

"We have this room booked until eleven, don't we?" Kempinski inquires calmly.

"I guess."

The field deputy then pulls over a metal chair and sits in front of Asciak.

"Well, Pol, the short version of the story is that your outstanding interrogation skills just won us a trip to the moon."

Satia also climb onto a metal chair. "That was great, Pol!" they exclaim.

"To the moon?" Asciak asks, unable to connect the dots. "I… I have never been to the moon."

"Trust me, you haven't been missing much. Make sure you pack some warm clothes, though," Kempinski comments casually.

"Okay… and the long version of the story?"

"The long version? Ah, yeah. Well, you might want to sit back down for that one."

INVESTIGATION DAY 5 (AFTERNOON)

In the detention center shared by Sectors 8C and 9C, inside one of the complex's interview rooms, Inspector Asciak listens to Kempinski piecing together the clues and inferences from their investigation that allegedly make a mission to the moon necessary. This video is recorded from the point of view of Special Unit Deputy Satia, who are perched on one of the chairs by the interrogation table. From his position in another of these chairs, Kempinski articulates his belief that the illegally imported cyborg in the warehouse was indeed Rainforest "Rainn" Kikinda, a ranked *Duplicate Conduit* competitor hailing from Byrgius. Sitting in front of Kempinski, Asciak shakes his head, unimpressed.

"Listen, Asciak, the other two players on that list are famous, highly ranked professionals," Kempinski says. "Household names in the *Conduit* community."

"So you're saying that Kikinda was not on their level?"

"Not just not on their level—he was a middling second-division player at best."

"Okay, Kempinski. Okay, that's clear and good to know. Still, the fact that one player stood out for you in Satia's list doesn't mean he's necessarily our guy. You're making an assumption. A plausible one, don't get me wrong, but an assumption nonetheless: the LUNA we saw in that video could be housing any of those three players!"

"Oh, come on! That Choksi creep pretty much confirmed it was Kikinda," mumbles Kempinski.

Slightly adjusting their position on the chair, Special Unit Deputy Satia point out the obvious: Choksi is not exactly a reliable source of information. Didn't the detainee also allege that Stan and Pol were in a romantic relationship?

Asciak seems anxious to drive his point home. "Look, I agree with you that Kikinda sounds like the odd one on that list," he says, "and yes, figuring out how he died and who paid for his rebirth is likely our best lead at the moment. But what I'm saying is that we shouldn't just buy into that theory hook, line, and sinker without further investigation."

Kempinski crosses his arms and quietly mutters something under his breath.

"But we need to start from somewhere, so let's roll with your hypothesis for now," Asciak continues. "So, if Kikinda is indeed the cyborg player that was illegally imported, couldn't this whole thing just be a plan to evade import taxes? I mean, could Vannevar simply be trying to make some extra chips by trading players without going through inter-sector checks and customs?"

Kempinski pauses to think. "That's unlikely," he declares a moment later. "Importing a player might take a long time because of clearance procedures, but it's not *that* expensive. I mean, compared with the cost of the shell and housing process, import tax is negligible."

Deputy Satia tilt their body to one side and vocalize their agreement with Kempinski. The smuggling scenario seems irrational to them, too, especially considering that the consequences for being caught would be various orders of magnitude greater than the meager potential financial gain.

Asciak nods. "Yeah, I see. And also, why would anyone in their right mind try to smuggle legal goods while using what is very likely a forged identity profile? Why try to cover up a small offense with a federal felony?"

Kempinski leans toward Asciak, supporting his weight on the table between them. "And get this, Inspector, when we looked for information on Kikinda's death on the security networks, all we could find was that he died on June 30 and that the circumstances of his death are classified."

"Classified? Still?! After a whole month?" Asciak asks incredulously.

"You heard that right. A security investigation must still be ongoing. Mark my words: something's fucked up with this Kikinda guy's situation."

Asciak says nothing for a while. He then asks Deputy Satia if anything about Kikinda's death has surfaced on the news networks. Anything at all. The Special Unit have already run some squeak-wide searches, but their queries yielded little to no information. This result did not trouble Deputy Satia, as it was compatible with the fact that no information about Kikinda's death had been officially released to the public. A couple of the least reputable sources, however, connected his death to a transport accident off the coast of West Antarctica—a private turbotransporter attempting an emergency water landing two hundred kilometers west of HOOS-MING TWO.

"That's probably bird shit," is all Kempinski has to say about that.

The room falls silent for a long while. Presumably with the intent of re-igniting the flow of ideas, Satia prompt Kempinski to explain why he thinks their investigation should continue on the moon, of all places. They have already heard the story back in the control room, suggesting that this request is meant to allow Inspector Asciak to get the full picture.

Kempinski looks at Asciak inquisitively. "Shall I explain?" he asks. The inspector shrugs and responds with a gesture inviting him to go ahead.

"Well, as I see it—and assuming that Kikinda is indeed the player inside that shell—there are two ways we can find out what happened to him. Option one: we wait until a report on his death is officially released on the security networks. Taking a passive stance in relation to our case might mean having to waste days, if not weeks. Option two: we take the initiative and reach out to the officers in charge of the Kikinda investigation."

"And why would we need to go to the moon for that? Wait, don't tell me that the case was assigned to them."

"It was. To a station in Byrgius, specifically. Unfortunately, not the one where I used to work."

"But how?! And is this why you find it unlikely that Kikinda died in Antarctica? I mean, the fact that a moon station is leading the investigation?"

"That is part of the reason, yeah. Think about it: if he really died a stone's throw off the coast of HOOS-TWO, why would a station on the moon be on this case? And also, what the fuck would Kikinda—a washed-out, average Joe of a player who had to keep working a day job to survive—be doing down here on a turbotransporter? I don't buy it."

"You think the two events are unrelated?"

"Kikinda's death and the transporter crash? Yeah, in terms of what took him out, I'd put my money on another dog."

Asciak pauses to think for a moment. "I see," he says, and then asks Kempinski if he happens to know what Kikinda's job was. "He was some kind of accountant or whatever," mumbles Kempinski.

Satia promptly correct the field deputy: according to his identity records, Kikinda was employed by a software company as a developer.

File ID: KC06
N.E. 330 – August 28, 12:07
[8C-SU Bakola (6584AR-4)]
(text automatically generated from video)

<Pol Asciak>: Can we pause the recording now, please?

<Elevii A. Tarkka ★☆☆>: Of course.
[Pauses the video]

<Pol Asciak>: Here's the other thing I wanted to comment on: what Kempinski *failed to mention* during this exchange...

Asciak again made use of the air quotes gesture.

<Pol Asciak>: What he should have flagged as a conflict of interest and a potential problem was his having been personally acquainted with Kikinda.

<Elevii A. Tarkka ★☆☆>: [Raising her eyebrows] His what?

<Pol Asciak>: Look, I'm not saying that they were close friends or anything, but I have testimonial evidence that Kempinski had previously met Kikinda on several occasions.

Bakola whirred strangely, as if the information also elicited some kind of emotional response in them.

<Pol Asciak>: You see, Kempinski used to live in Byrgius, too. And his former wife, Dr. Grace Tizzi, was a professional *Conduit* player.
[Pauses] Well, she still is. At the beginning of her career, for a couple of years or so, Tizzi played in Byrgius in the same regional division as Kikinda.

<Elevii A. Tarkka ★☆☆>: Mister Asciak, is it reasonable to assume that Kempinski's being acquainted with Kikinda is the reason he reacted the way he did earlier in the video? I'm referring to when he heard the player's name in relation to the case.

<Pol Asciak>: I... I guess so. You could put it that way, anyway.
[Pauses] In any case, what I want to emphasize at this point is that Kempinski withheld information not only about the case, but also regarding his personal involvement in it.

<Elevii A. Tarkka ★☆☆>: If what you're saying is true, it seems uncontestable to me that he behaved unprofessionally.

<Pol Asciak>: There's an audio recording in the repository of the Vannevar case where Dr. Tizzi says this explicitly. I mean, that Kempinski and Kikinda knew one another. You

could easily verify what I'm saying.

<Elevii A. Tarkka ★☆☆>: Are you referring to your conversation with her on the moon? Your lunch at... [Checks her LUNA]

<Pol Asciak>: Lamarck's. That's the place, yes.

<ELEVII'S LUNA>: Deputy, could you please copy that file to our repository?

<Elevii A. Tarkka ★☆☆>: [Pauses to think] In retrospect, do you know why Kempinski decided to act in bad faith?

<Pol Asciak>: Oh, I do.

<Elevii A. Tarkka ★☆☆>: [Drinks from her glass] [Gestures for Pol Asciak to continue]

<Pol Asciak>: I do. Because it is the very reason I'm sitting in front of you today as a person of interest in a murder case.

<Elevii A. Tarkka ★☆☆>: [Puts her glass down] [Stares at Pol Asciak] That isn't accurate. [Pauses] Mister Asciak, you are not presently a suspect. Following global security procedures, you are merely performing your deposition duties in an internal investigation.

<Pol Asciak>: [Shrugs] Po-tay-to, Po-tah-to.

<Merel Asciak>: [Inaudible]

<Elevii A. Tarkka ★☆☆>: I want to be absolutely clear on this point: you are a member of staff at this station, albeit temporarily suspended, and your mandatory deposition is instrumental in determining what happened to Kempinski. Nothing more, and nothing less.

<8C-SU BAKOLA>: It is done, Captain.

<Elevii A. Tarkka ★☆☆>: Going back to my question, could you share with us what you think Kempinksi's motives were? What was he trying to accomplish by withholding this information?

<Pol Asciak>: He was trying to protect Kikinda, Captain.

<Elevii A. Tarkka ★☆☆>: Protecting Kikinda from what, exactly?

<Pol Asciak>: [Scratching the back of his head] That... [Pauses] For that, we'll need to move to August 14th and view the video recorded in the back room of that shitty bar.

<Elevii A. Tarkka ★☆☆>: Clem's.

<Pol Asciak>: That's right, Clem's. I could talk about that now, or we could continue with this reconstruction chronologically. Take your pick. It makes no difference to me.

<NOTE> There is a rather long pause here. During this pause, I was silently wrestling with my desire to satisfy my curiosity at the expense of more systematic, serial work. </NOTE>

<Elevii A. Tarkka ★☆☆>: I... I think it would be better for us to continue following the events in the Vannevar case in a temporal sequence.
[Takes a deep breath] Is there anything else you would like to mention or comment upon before we move on?

<Pol Asciak>: Yeah, that... you know, that I wish Kempinski had been more trusting of me. But, yeah, I guess that was the point in the investigation when... well, when he decided I was no longer a partner to him...
[Trails off]

<Elevii A. Tarkka ★☆☆>: Please explain.

<Pol Asciak>: I think from that point onward, he started to see me as a sort of liability. A hazard both to himself and to Kikinda.

~~The room was suddenly very quiet. Merel Asciak poured some water into her empty glass and offered to fill mine as well. I smiled and nodded.~~ Having no follow-up questions, I proposed that we resume watching the video and conclude the morning session. The Asciaks both agreed. "Okay," says Inspector Asciak sitting in the interrogation room of the detention center. "Let's see if I understand the big picture here. In your hypothetical reconstruction, this Kikinda guy dies on June 30. Presumably on the moon, or perhaps in a crash landing near HOOS-MING TWO. We don't know for sure, right? Regardless of where it happened, we know that it did happen. Kikinda died. And when his body reached a medical facility, it was in good enough shape for him to take residence in a shell. How am I doing so far?"

Kempinski nods and then turns toward Satia and asks the Special Unit if they have any information about when Kikinda signed up for the rebirth program. On their screen interface, Satia bring up Kikinda's identity profile again. He had signed his authorization documents less than two months before his death. After Deputy Satia read out their findings, Kempinski comments that this timing is fucked up.

"Okay, but to wrap up," Asciak summarizes, "we have no information about where Kikinda died, where he was reborn, or who paid for the whole deal, presuming that it is indeed him inside that LUNA. What we know is that, about a week after his first death, that cyborg entered our sector illegally through some backdoor."

"Sounds about right," Kempinski remarks with a tone of finality.

Kempinski then leans back smugly into his metal chair. Satia point out that the player (whoever that might be) was likely kept in stasis mode for an extended period of time. Maybe they had been in that state ever since taking residence in their brand-new shell. This could explain the static shipping pose that the LUNA kept throughout its appearance in the warehouse video, despite being inhabited. The two officers do not, however, seem to assign any importance to the Special Unit's remark.

"Do you think it's possible that Kikinda is on the run?" asks Asciak. Kempinski frowns, unsure about where his colleague is going with this. The inspector tries again: "I don't know... what if someone wanted him dead?"

"You mean because he saw something he shouldn't have?" Kempinski appears to still be unsure where his partner is going.

"Either that, or because he made enemies inside a criminal organization."

"Or maybe because he was no longer useful to someone," Kempinski adds. "Well, should that be the case, we might want to try find Kikinda as soon as possible. That is, before they do."

Asciak agrees and remarks that it is funny how—in the speculative scenario where Kikinda is some kind of shell-bound fugitive—Egon Vannevar no longer features as a lowly smuggler, but as a heroic figure of sorts, someone who is putting himself in the line of fire to protect a friend in danger.

Kempinski taps his fingers on the table. "Okay, bub, but let's not go too far with this," he says. "First let's find out how Kikinda died, and where, and what kind of trouble he was in."

"Yeah, yeah." Asciak says, cutting the field deputy short. "And for that, we need to go to the moon." He stands up. "I get it."

Kempinski does not seem to mind the interruption. "Well," he counters complacently, "if you think we can advance the investigation more efficiently by focusing on the other two players on Satia's list instead, then let's just do that. Who knows, maybe the Byrgius people will manage to solve the case of Kikinda's death in the meantime."

"No," says Asciak while pinching the bridge of his nose. "No, I think you're right. We shouldn't waste time. We need to start by chasing our most promising lead. We need to get on a cruiser. Satia will check up on the other players while we're gone."

On their chair, Satia tilt their body to one side. Asciak walks up to the Special Unit and crouches to face their four frontal eyes at the same height. "Deputy," he says in a fatherly tone, "you know it would take us weeks to get you cleared for space travel. I am afraid you'll have to sit this one out."

Lowering themselves on their legs' actuators, Satia let out a subtle buzz.

> *<8C-SU BAKOLA>: It is indeed rare for Special Units to be authorized to leave the sector to which they belong, even when working on inter-tower investigations.*

Across the table from the inspector and the Special Unit, Kempinski also stands up. "All righty, then. If everyone is okay with this plan," he announces, "I propose to proceed as follows: yours truly will head back to the station this afternoon and take care of the paperwork and funding for our honeymoon. It might take us a day or two, but we should be on our way shortly. As suggested by Inspector Asciak, Satia will take care of the intel work on the other two players on the list and keep us notified of any progress or irregularities."

Satia assert their wholehearted agreement, although their posture seems to suggest something else.

"Is there anything I can do?" asks Asciak.

"You've already done plenty today, Inspector. The way you worked that guy... phew! What can you do? I don't know—take a rest, hit the gym... do whatever, but please give your older colleague a chance to feel useful, too!" Kempinski then smiles and adds, "Just don't make any plans for the rest of the week."

> <Pol Asciak>: [Raises a hand] Could you please pause the recording here? I want to comment on this part of the video.
>
> <Elevii A. Tarkka ★☆☆>: [Pauses the video] By all means.
>
> <Pol Asciak>: After the discussion we've just watched in this video, Kempinski did indeed go back to the station. He secured both the funding and the authorizations for our mission. He also made preliminary contact with the officers in Byrgius working on the case involving Kikinda.
>
> <Elevii A. Tarkka ★☆☆>: That sounds like efficient work.
>
> <Pol Asciak>: Too efficient, even. On that same afternoon, Stan also took care of something else. A task that we agreed on that might require some elaboration on my part.

Presumably feeling uncomfortable, Asciak shifted his weight in his chair.

> <Pol Asciak>: After leaving the detention facility—that is, on our way downtower to 8C—the team also agreed to request that a high-priority security alert be issued for Egon Vannevar.
>
> <Elevii A. Tarkka ★☆☆>: Why then? I mean, I agree it was

worth a shot, but your suspect might have left the sector weeks before!

<Pol Asciak>: Indeed, but you need to keep in mind that we had only started working the case 24 hours before, maybe even less. After watching the warehouse scene the previous day, I was already tempted to request a security alert on Vannevar, but we weren't sure we could prosecute him. Collecting undeclared goods is an offense, sure, but not in itself a criminal felony.

<Elevii A. Tarkka ★☆☆>: But things changed after you talked to Choksi, is what you're saying.

<Pol Asciak>: Yeah. In the wake of what happened in the detention facility, we felt that we had a somewhat clearer picture of Vannevar's involvement and that we could request an alert based on probable cause. As you can see, we were trying to go by the book.

<NOTE> I remember having to bite my tongue to refrain from commenting sarcastically on that last point. </NOTE>

<Elevii A. Tarkka ★☆☆>: What you're telling me is that, on that same afternoon—that is, still on July 30—Kempinski went to the station's Surveillance Office and requested a high-priority alert on your suspect.

<Pol Asciak>: Correct, you can check with them.

<Elevii A. Tarkka ★☆☆>: And I presume they used the warehouse footage to train the recognition software to recognize Egon Vannevar?

<Pol Asciak>: Given the absence of facial scans in the suspect's identity profile, I suppose Kempinski had no choice but to use that video as reference material, yes. [Pauses] I didn't ask him about that, though.

<8C-SU BAKOLA>: Captain, you two have been talking for over two and a half hours now.

<8C-SU BAKOLA>: Please be informed that Miss Asciak desperately needs a bathroom break, and you look like you could use some food. We suggest that we suspend the deposition for a bit.

<Pol Asciak>: Anyway, the reason I'm bringing this up... well, here's the thing—as you certainly know, the security operational manual mandates that security alert recognitions notify all staff members working on a case.

<Elevii A. Tarkka ★☆☆>: Indeed, it does.

<Pol Asciak>: Well, in this particular case, the only name listed to receive that alert was Kempinski's. This was in blatant violation of security directives on staff accountability and transparency in investigative procedures.

<Elevii A. Tarkka ★☆☆>: An infringement that you believe was deliberate?

<Pol Asciak>: I have no doubt it was. [Pauses] You see, Kempinski is friends with this guy at the Surveillance Office who—

<Elevii A. Tarkka ★☆☆>: [Interrupting] Do you know why he decided to exclude you and Satia from the recognition notifications for Vannevar?

<Pol Asciak>: For the same reason he did everything he did in this case—to keep Kikinda safe.
[Pauses] Satia and I realized something was off only a week later, as soon as we returned from the moon. It was actually Satia who found out about this.

<Elevii A. Tarkka ★☆☆>: Yes, and we'll get to that part—hopefully later today. For now, how would you feel about taking a short break for lunch?
[Looks at Merel Asciak] We've been going longer than usual. [Smiles]

<Merel Asciak>: [Abruptly] Yes, please!

<Pol Asciak>: [Shrugs] Sure, when do you want us back?

We agreed to reconvene in half an hour.

~~I ate my lunch in Room B1 with Captain Kutta. He had already eaten, but he seemed to value my company for some reason. I guess I decided to consume my bars there in the hope that he would share more information about what he had told me earlier that morning. Alas, the captain had nothing else to say to me concerning Miss Asciak's visit to Major Azucena. Talking to him about cyborg players also proved futile: he simply answered he often watched ranked competitions featuring them, but had never played against one himself. Those are professionals, he explained, and there is no reason for them to compete in local events.~~

During our lunch break, I received an unexpected urgent squeak-message. ~~The squeak alert made my LUNA vibrate and emit a pulsating bright red glow that, to no one's surprise, caught Uncle Rahman off guard.~~ The message was from Major Azucena. She was apologetically canceling our appointment. Something had come up, she wrote, and she would not be able to meet with me that afternoon. The chief offered to reschedule our meeting for the following day over lunch and asked me to confirm my availability at my "earliest convenience."

I messaged her back and agreed to meet with her the next day over lunch, ~~choosing one of the automated responses crafted by the rudimentary predictive intelligence of my LUNA.~~

<NOTE> I felt that I deserved a more informative explanation from her than "something came up," but I did not want my frustration to seep into my reply, potentially damaging our already uncertain relationship. </NOTE>

~~After lunch, just before we resumed the deposition, I squeaked Bakola to inform them about the rescheduled meeting.~~

We started the afternoon session of Pol Asciak's deposition a little after 2 PM. ~~The sun was setting, and the sky outside of Room B2~~

~~had a ferocious orange hue.~~ In this session, we managed to fully cover Asciak's account of the investigative team's security mission on the moon. For the reasons discussed above, Deputy Satia did not accompany them on their trip, which almost completely stunted our access to first-hand material on what happened during their time there. Because of the obvious security concerns, the two officers from Sector 8C were not authorized to record their conversations with the Byrgius Station staff investigating Kikinda's death. This meant that practically all the information I had about the moon segment of the Vannevar investigation came from Pol Asciak's testimony.

What Kempinski and Asciak found out in those days had a momentous impact on their case but hardly mattered for the current investigation. In Asciak's words, their moon mission was both a resounding success and a terrible mess. During the first day of their stay—that is, on August 10—the duo managed to ascertain, not without some difficulty, that Kikinda was indeed listed as one of the passengers of the turbotransporter that crashed off the coast of West Antarctica on the evening of June 30. According to the security officers in charge of investigating the player's death, Kikinda was an invited guest at an exclusive *Conduit* event. He had been summoned as a substitute player for an annual competition. This year, the competition was carried out in the Amundsen Sea in the newly renovated lobby of an underwater research facility located not far from HOOS-MING TWO. One of the patrons of the competition owned the facility and had offered to host the event, presumably as a way to show off their new, modern premises. A spokesperson for the organizing committee confirmed both that the event regularly took place on July 1 and that Kikinda was on the list of invited guests but, lamentably, did not attend.

<NOTE> When Asciak told me about this, I could not help but wonder what kind of organization would continue with an event of this type—a game—after one of the guests had just died in a tragic accident. Were they simply not informed about what happened, or was Kikinda's death considered inconsequential because he was a mere substitute player? Either way, I considered it all quite unseemly. </NOTE>

There was one part of Asciak and Kempinksi's moon expedition with verified recordings. That is the conversation the two security officers had with Dr. Grace Tizzi, Kempinski's former wife. Asciak mentioned these recordings during the morning session on the same day. Their lunch meeting took place on August 11 in a restaurant called Lamarck's. Meeting Dr. Tizzi was Kempinski's idea, but the choice of venue was not the field deputy's doing. It was his former wife who selected that fine-dining restaurant in central Byrgius, a venue whose prices were far beyond what a security station would be willing to reimburse for this kind of meeting. Dr. Tizzi was a regular there, which implied that she would be the one picking up the tab. Kempinski had apparently presented this to Asciak as an informal opportunity to gather additional information for their case. It was part of the job, the field deputy insisted. As a professional player, scholar, and game analyst, Tizzi was an invaluable source of knowledge about *Conduit*, its competitive scene, and the activities and subcultures orbiting around the ancient Fleeting game. ~~Kempinski's suggesting this meeting made sense to the inspector, who, although he never explicitly mentioned it, was evidently also curious to meet her, the woman who spent more than 20 years of her life with Kempinski and did so of her own volition.~~

According to Asciak's account of that meeting, the two officers got to Lamarck's with a half hour delay. ~~When they finally arrived, Dr. Tizzi was sitting alone at the booth she had reserved. She put down her cocktail glass, stood up, and greeted them warmly and without so much as a hint of irritation regarding their tardiness. Asciak said that Dr. Tizzi behaved as if she did not even notice that she was left waiting for over half an hour with no company but a bioluminescent jellyfish bobbing inside a large decorative tank. This was a detail that I could verify, as photos of the interior of Lamarck's revealed that curved glass jellyfish tanks doubled as partitions between some of the dining booths.~~

<NOTE> While recounting the events above, Asciak commented that Grace Tizzi was probably the most considerate person he ever met. Either that, or—knowing her former husband—she kept her expectations so abysmally low that she was indeed unfazed by how late they were. As I see it, these two possibilities are not mutually exclusive. </NOTE>

Asciak mentioned that Kempinski hugged his former wife. The field deputy then whispered something in her ear, and she smiled in return. Next, he introduced Asciak, who, after apologizing profusely and thanking Dr. Tizzi for being so generous with her time, asked her whether she would mind their meeting being recorded. According to Asciak's testimony, Tizzi was hesitant at first. People here on the moon are not used to being filmed, she allegedly explained. She also added that some of the regulars at Lamarck's are particularly old-fashioned and would find it uncouth for them to use cameras in the restaurant.

~~In the interrogation room where his deposition was taking place, Asciak commented that it was only then that he noticed that all the restaurant staff were basic humans: no cyborgs, no robotic prostheses, no enhancing visors, none of that stuff.~~

<NOTE> That felt strange to hear, and strangely discriminatory. I started to wonder if the people there would regard my hand—and the rest of me, by extension—as a threat to their privacy? </NOTE>

Unlike most public places in the megatowers on Earth, where security protocols imposed ubiquitous camera surveillance, Lamarck's did not seem to be monitored in any apparent way. To avoid trouble with the management and the other guests, Dr. Tizzi suggested opting for an audio log as a more discreet way to preserve their conversation for future reference. The inspector found that to be a suitable compromise and, I presume, then took an inconspicuous audio recorder out of his bag. As he was preparing to start recording, still according to Asciak's recounting, Kempinski practically grabbed a passing waiter by the arm to order an expensive bottle of Icelandic merlot.

File ID: KC10
N.E. 330 – August 11, 13:43:22
[SECURITY 8C-PORT 6 (R)] Audio 5
(text automatically generated from audio)

<Pol Asciak ☆☆☆>: Test... test...
[Pauses] Okay, this seems to be working.
[Clears his throat] All right. Allow me to thank you once again for meeting with us, Professor Tizzi. We are also

very grateful for your agreement to let us record this conversation.

<Grace Tizzi>: You are most welcome, officers. Maybe I should be the one thanking you for giving me an opportunity... excuse is perhaps the more precise variant here... to take a little break from writing.

<Pol Asciak ☆☆☆>: What are you working on, if I may ask?

<Grace Tizzi>: Oh, so kind of you to ask! It's a new feature for *Cond-Passion*. You might have heard of the magazine... the periodical. Writing articles for the popular press is a fun little thing I do besides... contiguously with... academic publishing.

<Pol Asciak ☆☆☆>: And what is the theme of the piece?

<Stanisław Kempinski ☆☆>: [Protesting] Pffft, as if you cared about stuff like that. Just get to the flipping point, Asciak!

<Grace Tizzi>: To answer your question, Inspector, my feature will be about our moral obligations to... well, about the question of our debt to the Fleeting. I intend to discuss the game of *Conduit* as a case in point to which the magazine's readership will be able to relate.

<Pol Asciak ☆☆☆>: That sounds like a fascinating topic.

<Grace Tizzi>: And as a title, I was thinking of "What We Owe the Dead," or something along those lines. It... it's a work-in-progress. You know, like pretty much everything.

<Pol Asciak ☆☆☆>: My colleague... well, Stan here told me that you also do analyses and live commentaries for *Duplicate Conduit* events and are a renowned figure in the game's competitive scene.

<Grace Tizzi>: It's what keeps me off the streets, one might say.
[Chuckles]

<Pol Asciak ☆☆☆>: [Laughs]

<Stanisław Kempinski ☆☆>: All right, all right. Enough pleasantries and small talk. Ask her about Kikinda, come on!

<NOTE> Kempinski's next sentence is nearly unintelligible. He is presumably not speaking to Asciak, but to the waiter who has just brought a bottle of wine to the table. From what I can understand, Kempinski seems to agree that he will taste the wine before it is served to the rest of the table. </NOTE>

<Pol Asciak ☆☆☆>: Yes, in fact we would be grateful for anything you could tell us about him. It's our understanding that you are acquainted with him, or at least that you were in the past.

<Stanisław Kempinski ☆☆>: [Smacks his lips] Ah, delightful!
[Pauses] Wine, anyone?

<Grace Tizzi>: Yes, please.
[Pauses] You see, Inspector, that was a long time ago, and Kikinda and I have never been close acquaintances, really. Our relationship, if we agree to call it such, never went beyond the *Conduit* table. It started and ended with the game.

<Pol Asciak ☆☆☆>: Then perhaps you could start by telling us what kind of player he was.

<Grace Tizzi>: [Sounding surprised] Was?

<Stanisław Kempinski ☆☆>: Oopsie!

<Pol Asciak ☆☆☆>: Well, fuck me.

<Stanisław Kempinski ☆☆>: [Chortles] Oh, don't worry about that, Inspector. Knowing this little bird here, she likely suspected the truth anyway. After all, why else would anyone send us all the way up here investigating a nobody of a player?

<Grace Tizzi>: [Interjecting] Stan is right. I did hear about his no-show at the Kleff Invitational, so I knew he must be in some kind of trouble. What I didn't know was how deep.

And... well, it looks like I just got my answer!
[Sighs]
[Pauses] Here, have some wine too.

<Pol Asciak ☆☆☆>: Th-thank you.
[Pauses] On the topic of that invitational game event. Have you heard of any other players who failed to attend, for whatever reason?

<Grace Tizzi>: I was invited but could not go because of... let's call it personal circumstances. In any case, I made sure to communicate my absence to the organizers with ample time in advance. A couple of hall of famers, though, simply failed to show up. Kleff is a large event, and absences due to illness are rather common, as are last-minute withdrawals. This is actually why organizers of events like that invite extra people who can serve as replacements... substitutes, like Kikinda.

<Pol Asciak ☆☆☆>: This Kleff Invitational... Is it an important tournament?

<Grace Tizzi>: It's a yearly event, and it is quite prestigious, yes. Significant, one could say. I wouldn't call it a tournament, though, given that the game's specific choreography... I mean, Kleff's unique format... does not encourage competitive play. I could explain in detail what sets *Covenant Conduit* apart from *Duplicate Conduit*, if you think it would potentially be relevant to your mission.

<Stanisław Kempinski ☆☆>: Spare us the pain, Grace.

The gurgling of more wine being poured can be heard over the faint background noise in the restaurant.

<Pol Asciak ☆☆☆>: Well, for now, we would be content with knowing whether it is common for semi-professionals and second-division players to be invited as substitutes for these kinds of events.

<Grace Tizzi>: Let's say it's relatively infrequent. Sporadic, if you will.

<Pol Asciak ☆☆☆>: I see. And going back to an earlier point in our conversation, is there anything you can tell us

about Kikinda as a player?

<Grace Tizzi>: As a player? Hmmm... he is... he *was* a second-division player whom I met at the dawning of... at the beginning of my career, Inspector. That was when Rainforest and I played in the same league here in Byrgius. I wasn't married to Stan at the time, but we had started dating. Your dear colleague would often come to see me play in local competitions.

<Pol Asciak ☆☆☆>: Is there anything you can tell us about Kikinda's playstyle or his table manners? Anything you remember, really.

<Grace Tizzi>: Hmm... Kikinda was a fairly average player, if memory serves. Not particularly inspired or inventive in his maneuvers... in his vision. He was, however, unafraid to take chances, so he would go for any opportunity, no matter how slim his chances.
[Pauses] You talked with him a few times, too, didn't you, Stan?

<Stanisław Kempinski ☆☆>: I was in the audience, so I guess I didn't have quite the same level of engagement you had. But, yes, I must have exchanged a few words with him between rounds and during breaks.

<Pol Asciak ☆☆☆>: Hmm...

In the interrogation room, Asciak asked me to pause the recording at this point so that he could underscore the fact that—as he anticipated during the morning session—Tizzi's interview confirmed that Kempinski and Kikinda had met in the past, which Kempinski's reluctant admission also confirmed, albeit in a strategically downplayed fashion. I agreed with Asciak that he had accurately represented what was said at Lamarck's and proposed that we continue listening to the recording. ~~At that point in the deposition session, the sky outside the megatower was completely dark.~~

<Pol Asciak ☆☆☆>: Did he have problems with drugs—did you ever hear anything like that? Money issues, perhaps?

<Grace Tizzi>: Not that I recall.

<Stanisław Kempinski ☆☆>: Grace, darling, I know you're not the kind to gossip, but we're desperately looking for a working hypothesis. Something to start from. Anything.

<Grace Tizzi>: In that case, there might have been some allegations... stories about him having a gambling problem in the past. But that was many years ago, and I wouldn't give those kinds of rumors any weight... any importance. You wouldn't believe the amount of filth—pardon my language—that our relatively small community is capable of spewing.

<Stanisław Kempinski ☆☆>: All righty, that's already something we can work with. [Sound of a chair being pushed back from the table] And now, ladies and germs, I hope you will excuse me. This old man needs to powder his nose.

<Pol Asciak ☆☆☆>: [Sounding confused] Oh... okay?
<Grace Tizzi>: Is it a new habit of his to declare... to publicly announce his bathroom breaks?

<Pol Asciak ☆☆☆>: I don't know how to answer that question, Professor.

In the passage that follows, Dr. Tizzi is speaking to a server. In it, she likely turned her head away from Asciak's recording device, as her volume is significantly lower than in the rest of the conversation.

<Grace Tizzi>: Hello, yes. Yes, I think we're ready. Could we see the lunch menu, please? Thank you. [Pauses] Are you hungry, Inspector?

<Pol Asciak ☆☆☆>: I... I guess I could eat.

<Grace Tizzi>: That's wonderful. The cuisine here is unparalleled! I hope you'll keep your appetite... your interest in food.

<Pol Asciak ☆☆☆>: Wh-what do you mean?

<Grace Tizzi>: I mean once you realize that Stan is not coming back.

<Pol Asciak ☆☆☆>: You must be joking.

<Grace Tizzi>: Pol... may I call you Pol?

<Pol Asciak ☆☆☆>: I...

<Grace Tizzi>: Look, my relationship with my former husband is like a... say, a foreign language. A language with which I am no longer completely familiar. [Pauses] The analogy... the simile here is that I might not be able to "speak Stan" anymore, but I can still read him. [Pauses] And that man is gone.

<Pol Asciak ☆☆☆>: Gone where?!

<Grace Tizzi>: I'm not sure, Inspector. My guess would be a melancholic bender in some disreputable hole in the wall.

<Pol Asciak ☆☆☆>: You must be wrong. Stan will return any minute now.
<Grace Tizzi>: I bet you he won't.

He did not.

INVESTIGATION DAY 6 (MORNING)

August 29 – SS8C

~~On the final morning of his deposition hearing, Pol Asciak was sitting alone on the bench in the hallway, Room B0, almost an entire hour before we had agreed to meet. Freshly shaven and evidently eager to start the session, he politely stood up when I came out of the elevator. He wished me a good morning, and I nodded with a thin-lipped smile and wondered where Merel Asciak was. I then walked into the interview room alone and closed the door behind me.~~

As usual, I went through the notes and questions I had prepared for the upcoming deposition session before Deputy Bakola joined me in Room B2. I even had time to listen to the lunchtime conversation between Asciak and Tizzi again, starting from the beginning and including the exchange that took place after Kempinski left Lamarck's. That part of the audio recording, ~~I will call it "the second half,"~~ did not, however, contain useful information for the advancement of their case. I nevertheless believe that it is worth mentioning here because it revealed something marginally relevant to my own investigation. Here, I am referring to an aspect of Asciak's character that I had not witnessed until this point in the investigation: in a few parts of the conversation, the inspector does not seem to be exclusively concerned with himself and his work. I will thus provide a brief account of the exchange below.

After Asciak and Tizzi finished the first course of the meal, their conversation circled back to the *Conduit* invitational in which Kikinda was supposed to take part. It was then that inspector Asciak surprised me by explicitly manifesting his discomfort with the idea that the event proceeded as planned, in full, and according to schedule, as if nothing tragic had occurred. Surely, the rest of the invited players must have been informed about the accident, he commented. Did they just continue playing as if nothing horrific had happened? Asciak openly asked the scholar whether such callousness was a common trait of *Conduit* players. Tizzi responded to the inspector's question with a straightforward statement delivered in a tone without any malice or ill intention— one could ask the same question regarding security officers, she said.

<NOTE> Asciak did not react to this. Not in a way that was captured by the audio recording device in any case. </NOTE>

Again, I do not feel that Tizzi was trying to be dismissive or cynical. Almost immediately, in fact, she clarified that a certain degree of cynicism might be something that comes with playing *Duplicate Conduit*, but also happens to be the case in Asciak's own line of work. ~~She then took the Inspector's question as an opportunity to present additional contextual information about the invitational event. Kleff, she explained, is unique in its importance for the *Conduit* community and can be seen as more of a celebration of the game than a competitive event. It is a "rekindling ceremony" of sorts, she added, that has been organized and played on the first day of July every year for the last 200 years or so, which corresponds to when our society's version of the Fleeting game reached the relatively stable ludic form we know today. Kleff symbolizes our collective carrying forward of the torch that was passed to us by the Fleeting, Tizzi continued.~~

<NOTE> I could not help noticing that, when talking about *Conduit*, the scholar had a clear penchant for fire-related metaphors. </NOTE>

~~The game promotes a certain "mode of thinking," she argued. The thoughts and values that it invites clearly transcend the needs and timescale of our species and are worth preserving—even just for that reason. The ritual elements of *Conduit* are thus central to our relationship with the game, Tizzi concluded, and they matter more to our community than the struggles and misfortunes that might befall its individual players.~~

~~Asciak sounded receptive, even sympathetic, to the perspective Dr. Tizzi was presenting. The importance of Kleff for the community of *Conduit* players was also not lost on him.~~ Still, the inspector's thoughts and opinions about what happened at the event did not seem to change during the conversation.

<NOTE> Dr. Tizzi then offered a few formal details concerning the "Covenant" version of the game. In contrast to *Duplicate Conduit*, this ritual form is played semi-collaboratively and on a much larger board than the regular tournament version. *Covenant Conduit* also features a special set of playing cards with an additional suite of Fleeting symbols that is not used in regular competitive play. </NOTE>

The rest of their exchange was of no importance to the Vannevar case and is also irrelevant to my own case. ~~I sped through most of it. Thanks to Asciak's curiosity in the second half of that audio recording, I happened to learn something mildly unexpected about Kempinski's personal life. According to his former wife, he felt uncomfortable in his role as a married man and did not enjoy sharing a living space with her. Dr. Tizzi mentioned something about her allegedly "cramping his style." That was not the part that surprised me. What I did not expect to hear was that Kempinski was the one who finally filed for divorce.~~

As I was wrapping up my review of the recording of the conversation with Dr. Tizzi, Deputy Bakola entered the interrogation room, with a few minutes still left before the start of the session. ~~They appeared to be in a good mood.~~ I asked the Special Unit to please leave the door open so the Asciaks could come in whenever they were ready to begin what we expected to be the last session of Pol Asciak's deposition. I knew we had another busy day ahead of us, and, worrying that I might forget to do it later, I asked the Special Unit to try to schedule a first session with Egon Vannevar. According to protocol, that should be our next investigative step, and so I asked Deputy Bakola to try to book it as soon as they managed to obtain all the necessary authorizations. They agreed with the peculiar full-bodied nod of Special Units. A few minutes later, the Asciaks entered the interview room. ~~Merel was wearing a sweet perfume that reminded me of apricots.~~

> File ID: KC07
> N.E. 330 – August 29, 09:58
> [8C-SU Bakola (6584AR-4)]
> (text automatically generated from video)

<Elevii A. Tarkka ★☆☆>: All right. I presume this is going to be the final session of Mister Asciak's deposition concerning his involvement in the Vannevar case. [Pauses] The date is August 29th, 330. It is close to 10 in the morning, and, as in all our previous sessions, Merel Asciak is in attendance as Pol Asciak's legal representative. Welcome to you both, and thank you once again for being here. [Takes a deep breath] Now, the final piece of evidence we discussed last afternoon, before closing yesterday's session, was the audio file of your conversation with Dr. Tizzi. [Pauses] Is there anything that you'd like to add concerning that file? Anything that you believe was not covered—or not covered in sufficient depth?

<Pol Asciak>: Not really, no. [Pauses] Well, actually, maybe that, after my conversation with Dr. Tizzi— that is, off the record—she shared with me the squeak contact of someone she knew who was on the organization committee for this year's Kleff Invitational. A district lawyer from Grimaldi City. [Pauses] I found that very thoughtful of her.

<Elevii A. Tarkka ★☆☆>: Thoughtful in the sense that she wanted to assist you in using the rest of your time on the moon productively? Is that what you're saying?

<Pol Asciak>: Precisely. She didn't have to do that.

<Elevii A. Tarkka ★☆☆>: Nor was she under any

obligation to meet with the two of you in the first place, for that matter. In any case, did you get in touch with Tizzi's contact?

<Pol Asciak>: I did. I squeak-called the lawyer later on that same day. She didn't try to hide the fact that she was not thrilled to speak to me. Our call was very brief. She... well, she informed me that she had already told everything she knew about what happened at Kleff to the security officer who had questioned her two weeks earlier. That was at an official deposition at Byrgius station, and it was on record. Why, then, the lawyer asked, was she being questioned again?

<Elevii A. Tarkka ★☆☆>: Did you explain that you couldn't access her testimony because the case contained classified information about an ongoing investigation?

<Pol Asciak>: Yes, of course. But she replied to that by saying that my clearance level wasn't her problem. She made the additional point that she was also under no obligation to answer any of my questions.
[Sighs] And, you know... that was that.

<Elevii A. Tarkka ★☆☆>: Fair enough.

<Pol Asciak>: On the next morning, I also succeeded in getting in touch with a professional player who I knew was among the guests invited to the event. That was a longer squeak-call. The player was friendly and willing to help but claimed not to be personally acquainted with Kikinda. He said he had loved this year's Kleff and described the lavish underwater venue in great detail. In his account, the game went very smoothly, and he was happy with the final configuration his table reached. Again, though, none of that was of any use in terms of moving our case forward.

<Elevii A. Tarkka ★☆☆>: Hmm.

<Pol Asciak>: By the way, if you think it might be useful, I could provide the names and contact information for both of these individuals.

<Elevii A. Tarkka ★☆☆>: I don't think that's necessary, but thank you for offering.

[Pauses] Going back to Kempinski, do you remember when you next saw him?

<Pol Asciak>: I do. You see, I tried to call him multiple times, but his squeak was always off or unreachable. The next time we met in person was... it was at the Byrgius spaceport.

<Elevii A. Tarkka ★☆☆>: Boarding your cruiser back to HOOS-MING ONE?

<Pol Asciak>: About two hours before boarding time, give or take. When I arrived, Stan was sitting alone at our gate. The place was still almost deserted, and he was slouched across two seats, half-asleep.

<Elevii A. Tarkka ★☆☆>: Did you confront him at that time?

<Pol Asciak>: Well, I sat down next to him. [Pauses] He reeked of booze like you wouldn't believe. I was obviously very disappointed in him. And angry, but I didn't want to make a scene.

<8C-SU BAKOLA>: For your information, Captain, there seems to be an issue with scheduling the interrogation with Egon Vannevar. We do not have sufficient time at this moment to determine exactly what the issue is, but it might have something to do with our clearance level.

<Pol Asciak>: I managed to keep my cool. As calmly as I could, I asked Kempinski what he was thinking, behaving like that. Did he think our case was a game? Did we come here just to give him an excuse to get drunk on the station's dime?

<8C-SU BAKOLA>: Perhaps you could try to schedule the interrogation yourself later. Your security profile might have access rights or hidden features that ours does not.

<ELEVII'S LUNA>: Much appreciated, Deputy. Will do.

<Pol Asciak>: In response, Kempinski burped and mumbled that I had better leave him alone.

<Elevii A. Tarkka ★☆☆>: Charming.

<Pol Asciak>: At that point, I was THIS CLOSE to punching his stupid yellow teeth in.

<Merel Asciak>: Ahem... [Raising her index finger] May I?

<Elevii A. Tarkka ★☆☆>: [Speaking to Merel Asciak] Sure, Miss Asciak, go ahead.

<Merel Asciak>: Allow me to clarify that my client meant that as hyperbole. He was simply employing a figure of speech for effect. I would also like to put it on the record that, his occasional passionate outbursts notwithstanding, Mister Asciak is not known to have a quick temper. Nor does he have a history of acting violently toward colleagues or associates.

<Elevii A. Tarkka ★☆☆>: Thank you for the clarification.

<Pol Asciak>: Yes, thank you, Merel. [Touches Merel Asciak's forearm]

<Elevii A. Tarkka ★☆☆>: [Speaking to Pol Asciak] Back to August the 13th, how did you react when Kempinski told you to leave him alone?

<Pol Asciak>: Again, I felt angry. It took considerable effort to keep my emotions in check. I ground my teeth. Eventually, I got up and sat somewhere else. Oh, I might also have told him to go and get fucked.

<Elevii A. Tarkka ★☆☆>: Right. So, when is it that the two of you *did* get to talk about the case and, I presume, his behavior?

<Pol Asciak>: Wait. Something else happened before we got to that part.

<Elevii A. Tarkka ★☆☆>: Okay...

<Pol Asciak>: As I was sitting on my own in another area of the gate, trying to calm down, I witnessed something very curious. A sickly looking middle-aged man with a beard

walked up to where Kempinski was dozing off. I couldn't hear what he said, but he seemed to be inquiring as to whether the seat next to Kempinski was free. Kempinski straightened himself up and gestured for the other man to go ahead and sit down.

<Elevii A. Tarkka ★☆☆>: Didn't you say that the gate was still quite empty at the time?

<Pol Asciak>: It was. Since there were plenty of available seats, I found it strange that this man made the conscious decision to sit right next to Kempinski. Especially considering Kempinski's smell, but anyway… [Pauses, appearing to think] Ah, and there's another detail about the bearded man that captured my attention: he was wearing a long-sleeved shirt with a large picture of a little piggy dressed as a construction worker on the front.

<Elevii A. Tarkka ★☆☆>: You mean like a vignette or…

<Pol Asciak>: Sort of a vignette, yeah. In any case, the bearded man started talking to Kempinski. I was surprised to see that, instead of telling him to shut his hairy hole, Kempinski was genuinely interested in what the stranger was saying. He even appeared to be asking questions in return. All this lasted, say, three minutes, maybe less. After that, the man in the piggy shirt got up and unsteadily walked away.

<Elevii A. Tarkka ★☆☆>: Never to come back again, I suppose.

<Pol Asciak>: Yeah, he left for good. [Pauses] And Kempinski just slouched back in his seat as if nothing out of the ordinary had happened.

<Elevii A. Tarkka ★☆☆>: Hmm.

<Pol Asciak>: To answer your previous question, he and I finally got to talk aboard the cruiser back home. According to Kempinski, the bearded man was a former colleague of his. You know, from back in the days when Kempinski was a security officer in Byrgius. Although not directly involved with investigating Kikinda's death, this former colleague was apparently privy to classified information about that case. Information that we could not otherwise have accessed.

<Elevii A. Tarkka ★☆☆>: With reference to what you said yesterday evening, would you qualify what you've just described as doing investigative work "by the book"?

<Pol Asciak>: I certainly would not, Captain.

<Elevii A. Tarkka ★☆☆>: And did Kempinski share with you what the former colleague told him?

<Pol Asciak>: He did. The man in the tacky shirt told Kempinski something crucial about the accident in West Antarctica that had killed Kikinda. Apparently, there were *two* passengers inside the turbotransporter that crash-landed into the ocean, not just one. Two players, both picked up at the HOOS-MING TWO spaceport, and both heading to the underwater research facility for the *Conduit* event. According to Kempinski's former colleague, neither player had survived the accident.

<Elevii A. Tarkka ★☆☆>: What was the name of the other player?

<Pol Asciak>: Mumbi.

<Elevii A. Tarkka ★☆☆>: Mumbi?

<Pol Asciak>: Onfime Mumbi, the Duplicate *Conduit* hall of famer.

<Elevii A. Tarkka ★☆☆>: The name... it sounds familiar.
<Pol Asciak>: He was quite the famous figure. You probably heard about the enshrinement ceremony the *Conduit* Association held for his retirement a couple of months ago.

<Elevii A. Tarkka ★☆☆>: I can't say that I did. [Pauses] Did the bearded man know whether anyone on board the turbotransporter survived the impact?

<Pol Asciak>: Yes. Apparently, the two pilots and a steward made it out alive. With only minor injuries, in fact. Kempinski's former colleague said that the "Mumbi case" relied for the most part on the eyewitness testimony of the

three survivors... and, of course, on the telemetric data and squeak communications recorded by the HOOS-MING TWO spaceport.
[Pauses] The witnesses allegedly reported that Kikinda was still conscious when they evacuated the transporter. The other player, alas, was not as lucky.

<Elevii A. Tarkka ★☆☆>: Does that mean that Mumbi died upon impact or that they did not manage to rescue him from the wreck?

<Pol Asciak>: That... that was not clear. Kempinski mentioned that this former colleague didn't have complete access to information about the case, but that he had presented it as a fact that Mumbi had been aboard the transporter, and that his body had sunk together with its crashed fuselage.

<Elevii A. Tarkka ★☆☆>: Okay. This might not be very relevant to the present case, but do you happen to know if Kempinski's conversation partner explained why Mumbi's case was classified to begin with? Let me rephrase that. Did the bearded man indicate that Byrgius station had reason to believe the crash wasn't an accident?

<Pol Asciak>: Yeah, from what I understood, they're investigating it as an intentional act. As murder.

<Elevii A. Tarkka ★☆☆>: I see. Now, going back to your own investigation...

<Pol Asciak>: [Interrupting] Yeah, going back to our investigation, Kempinski and I were not coming back home empty-handed. We still didn't know who had paid for Kikinda's rebirth, but the alleged presence of Mumbi on that transporter answered many of the other questions we had. You see, Mumbi was not only a famous player, but also a rather controversial public figure because of his political views. It was reasonable to assume that he had enemies and that some of those enemies might have been happy to take Mumbi's honorific invitation to this year's Kleff as an opportunity to get rid of him.

<Elevii A. Tarkka ★☆☆>: And in this scenario, Kikinda's death would feature as what? Collateral damage?

<Pol Asciak>: Yeah. At the time, I thought of Kikinda as an unlucky bystander who got caught in the crossfire. This possibility had the additional advantage of explaining why someone would be willing to spend money to bring Kikinda back as a cyborg.

<Elevii A. Tarkka ★☆☆>: Are you implying that a third party actively saved Kikinda's life because he witnessed Mumbi's murder?

<Pol Asciak>: Correct, that was one of my working hypotheses.

<Elevii A. Tarkka ★☆☆>: Why would that be necessary? I mean, unlike Kikinda, the crash survivors would not need to be reborn in an exorbitantly expensive shell to allow them to testify. Why not rely on the testimony of the pilots and steward instead?

<Pol Asciak>: I can explain why there was reason to suspect the steward and the pilots of being directly involved in Mumbi's assassination if you think that will give you useful information about the context. I'm not sure how that information would be relevant to your investigation, though.

<Elevii A. Tarkka ★☆☆>: I... that's—

<Pol Asciak>: [Interrupting] In any case, none of that actually matters. That theory was wrong. It was simply one of several possible ways to combine the information we had at the time.
[Shakes his head] One that Kempinski led me to believe was likely.

<Elevii A. Tarkka ★☆☆>: Could you elaborate on that? If that's not what actually happened, then how did Kikinda die?

<Pol Asciak>: I... for that, we need to get into what happened on the following day, Captain.

<Elevii A. Tarkka ★☆☆>: [Takes a deep breath] [Looks at her cybernetic hand] Okay, but there's one more thing I need to ask before we talk about your raid of Clem's

bar. A couple of days ago, during one of our deposition sessions, you mentioned that, on your cruiser ride back home, you confronted Kempinski on themes related to leadership and mutual trust.

<Pol Asciak>: Yes, that's right.

<Elevii A. Tarkka ★☆☆>: To some extent, I believe that you have already presented the reasons for your dissatisfaction, but could you please go through that exchange in detail?

<Pol Asciak>: Sure, I guess. [Shrugs] After Kempinski shared the new information concerning the Vannevar case he got from his former colleague, I called him out on a number of issues related to his professional behavior. You know, his drinking on the job, his withholding information about his acquaintance with Kikinda, and the way he just bailed on me halfway through our moon mission. I told him that I found these things unacceptable and that he gave me no choice but to report him to Azucena.
[Turns toward Tarkka] I hope you understand that I'm not used to cutting corners and bending truths. I... again, I wanted to work in a team that valued transparency and personal accountability. I wanted to do things right.

<8C-SU BAKOLA>: *As an interesting note, Stan once told us that there are three ways to do security work: the right way, the wrong way, and the Kempinski way.*

<Pol Asciak>: In response, Kempinski just nodded and then said something along the lines of "You do you, bub," turned away from me in his seat, and fell asleep leaning against the window of the cruiser.

Pol Asciak was then silent for a while. We were reaching the end of his testimony, with only one day in their investigation left to cover. I was confident that we could be done by lunchtime, which was when my meeting with the station chief was scheduled to take place. I decided to take advantage of the anticlimactic moment in Pol Asciak's story to propose a short break before the final stretch of the deposition. No one in the room objected.

<NOTE> During our breather, I asked Deputy Bakola if Kempinski had ever explained what he meant by "the Kempinski way." The Special Unit shrugged and replied that doing security work "the Kempinski way" was pretty much the same as doing it wrong, just more entertaining or something like that. </NOTE>

When we resumed 15 minutes later, Pol Asciak told us about their return trip from the HOOS-MING ONE spaceport to Sector 8C. Although this trip was mostly uneventful, their ride downtower took several hours because of a series of excruciatingly slow inter-sector checks. The two security officers thus reached their respective homes late in the evening.

On the following day, as prescribed by security protocols, both officers were required to take a day off. Because he had not managed to get any sleep on the moon cruiser, Asciak was apparently hit by moon-lag in a way that was particularly severe. As soon as he got home, he told us, Asciak silenced his squeak notifications and fell asleep without even changing clothes. It was past noon on the following day when a tenacious buzzing woke the inspector.

> File ID: KC07
> N.E. 330 – August 29, 11:25
> [8C-SU Bakola (6584AR-4)]
> (text automatically generated from video)

<Pol Asciak>: I was very confused. I didn't anticipate that moon-lag would be such a pain. It... it took me a while to realize that I wasn't dreaming and that I actually was receiving an urgent call from work. I knew I had silenced my squeak, but it was ringing anyway, which added to my disorientation. Eventually, I managed to pick up the call. Deputy Satia were on the other end of the line. The Special Unit were at the security station and using an override code to contact me. They asked me how I was doing and inquired as to whether it was a good time to talk. I must have mumbled something incoherent in response.

<Elevii A. Tarkka ★☆☆>: Go on.

<Pol Asciak>: Well, then I asked whether whatever they needed could wait until the next day. I thought Satia just wanted to update me on their independent investigation. You know, regarding the other players on that list.

<Elevii A. Tarkka ★☆☆>: Yes. Please continue.

<Pol Asciak>: Well, they told me it wasn't about that. It was about Kempinski.
[Pauses] I felt dizzy and tried to sit up in bed. Remember the security alert that was placed on Egon Vannevar?

<Elevii A. Tarkka ★☆☆>: The one that your Surveillance Office unlawfully set to notify Kempinski's squeak exclusively?

<Pol Asciak>: Yes, exactly. As I already mentioned, Kempinski and I were instructed not to come into work the day, so when Deputy Satia saw Kempinski at the station early that morning, they found it very strange.

<Elevii A. Tarkka ★☆☆>: Yes, coming to work early in the morning when he had the day off also doesn't quite match my mental image of Field Deputy Kempinski.

<Pol Asciak>: The Special Unit told me that Kempinski was wearing civilian clothes and that he was in a rush, which is also uncharacteristic of him. Soon after, Satia told me, Kempinski walked directly into Azucena's office, without knocking, slamming the door behind him.

Deputy Bakola let out an odd buzz—possibly a sign of heightened attention.

<Pol Asciak>: A few minutes after that, Satia saw him leave the station. Curious about what was going on, the Special Unit accessed the security mainframe and checked Kempinski's latest activities on the security network. It didn't take them long to piece the puzzle together: that very morning, Kempinski was alerted of multiple recognition notifications for Vannevar. Our suspect was still in Sector 8C.

<Elevii A. Tarkka ★☆☆>: Go on.

<Pol Asciak>: The detection points he received were concentrated in an area close to the center of the column. Naturally, Satia assumed that Kempinski was heading there.

<Elevii A. Tarkka ★☆☆>: They thought he was pursuing Vannevar.

<Pol Asciak>: My head was swimming. Why would he exclude us from the alert notifications in the first place? What could he possibly have told the chief? And why chase Vannevar alone and risk blowing the entire investigation? [Pauses] I was still in bed, trying to make sense of what I had just heard. Then, Satia urged me to get up. We needed to head there, too, they urged. And quickly. The Special Unit sent me the rendezvous coordinates via squeak. I was supposed to meet them near where Vannevar's face had been picked up by the automated detection software. And, by the way, everything I'm telling you now can be verified in Satia's footage for the day, as well as in the log of our squeak communications.

<Elevii A. Tarkka ★☆☆>: Did you reach the location indicated by Deputy Satia directly from your habitation?

<Pol Asciak>: I did. Still wearing the same clothes from the previous day, I pretty much ran there. Going there directly from my apartment was the quickest option for me. When I arrived at the intersection Satia had indicated, the Special Unit were already there and had apparently been waiting for me for some time, quietly patrolling the area. I don't know how familiar you are with this sector, but the last crisis was really rough on us, economically speaking. With the worsening of the metal availability crisis, hardly anyone lives in the column center these days.

<NOTE> He was referring to the fact that tramlines are no longer operational in the area and that the tram rails had long been stripped and sold, together with the metal components of most buildings in the area. In Satia's footage, the column center looked desolate and forsaken. In a sense, it was not surprising for someone to choose this place to lay low and out of sight. </NOTE>

<Pol Asciak>: Anyway, while Satia were waiting for me, they had filed a request with our Surveillance Office for both of us to also be notified of any new hits on Egon Vannevar. Their request was approved within minutes, and, sure enough, we soon received an alert. A new detection point was blinking on Satia's map. They told me it was only two blocks away from where we were.

<Elevii A. Tarkka ★☆☆>: So, I'm guessing that this brings us to the part where you hid inside the entrance hall of an abandoned building and waited for Vannevar to show up.

<Pol Asciak>: Indeed, we were right in front of that squalid little bar. And when Vannevar finally walked down the street, Kempinski was with him. I guess I felt relieved to see he was still alive, but I didn't expect to see them walking down the street together. My best guess as to what was happening was that Vannevar was armed and leading the dance, so to speak—forcing Kempinski to go with him against his will.

<8C-SU BAKOLA>: In the video of this part of the incident, this is where Pol calls Stan a "huge pile of bird shit." An instant classic.

<Pol Asciak>: Vannevar must have a knife, I thought, or even a taser. We watched them enter the bar and disappear from sight. Unfortunately, Deputy Satia were unable to confirm whether either Vannevar or Kempinski was carrying a weapon.

<Elevii A. Tarkka ★☆☆>: Did it occur to you at that point that Clem's could have been a hideout of some sort? A place where Vannevar had friends and a location where he felt safe? After all, the bar's owner had a criminal record of his own.

<Pol Asciak>: I didn't know about Mister Young's own criminal record at the time, of course, but I did consider that possibility, yes.

<Elevii A. Tarkka ★☆☆>: And, yet, you still decided to raid the bar, with no reinforcements. Just the two of you.

<Pol Asciak>: I felt that I didn't have much of a choice in

that situation. I had to act in the interest of my partner's safety. Remember I suspected that Vannevar was threatening Kempinski.

<Elevii A. Tarkka ★☆☆>: Hmm... [Pauses, appearing to think] I suggest that we let Satia's video recording cover the events that followed. As you know, there is blood in the scene, and we might see some, depending on how far we go into the recording. Is this okay with you?

<Pol Asciak>: Just go ahead.

<Merel Asciak>: [Appearing to hesitate] Is... this might be tough for my client to watch. Perhaps Pol could wait outside of the room while we...

<Pol Asciak>: [Interrupting] It's going to be alright, Merel. It will be fine.

After making sure that everyone was comfortable enough with the proposition, I played the scene at Clem's on the room's window-sized screen. On the screen's curved surface, we watched Asciak swiftly approach the bar's door, barge inside, threaten Clement Young, and eventually walk to the door of one of the establishments' back rooms. I paused the video just before Asciak walked through the door to the back room, alone.

<Elevii A. Tarkka ★☆☆>: Mister Asciak, we have just watched you instruct Deputy Satia to remain in the main area of the bar with Clement Young.

<Pol Asciak>: Yes, and this is textbook stuff. We needed to both keep an eye on Mister Young and make sure that no one fled the bar, at least not via its front door.

<Elevii A. Tarkka ★☆☆>: Yes, I'm familiar with the procedure, and my observation was not meant as a criticism of your decision as the higher-ranking officer. I simply wanted to emphasize that this course of action led to our not having a video recording of what happened inside that back room.

<Pol Asciak>: That is correct.

<Elevii A. Tarkka ★☆☆>: In reconstructing the events in question, we will thus have to rely on your testimony. And on the testimony that Egon Vannevar and Clem Young will provide in the next few days, clearly. So, Mister Asciak, please recount your side of the story.

<Pol Asciak>: [Takes a deep breath] Okay, yes. [Pauses] As you could tell from the video, I was already on edge as I entered the bar.

<Elevii A. Tarkka ★☆☆>: Understandably so.

<Pol Asciak>: And I got even tenser when I was about to go through that door, unarmed and unsure of what was waiting for me inside. When I stepped in, I was ready for a physical confrontation.
[Pauses] Behind the door, however, was just a narrow and dimly lit hallway. As quietly as I could manage, I walked down that corridor until I reached a larger room, a private drinking space of sorts. There, as far as I could tell, Kempinski and Vannevar were alone, sitting on the same side of an old table. They were talking.

<Elevii A. Tarkka ★☆☆>: How did Kempinski react when he saw you walk in?

<Pol Asciak>: When I stepped into the light, Kempinski stared at me, clearly in shock. You know, like he had just seen a ghost or something.

<NOTE> Clearly, Kempinski did not anticipate being followed. I wonder if, at that point, he wished that he had opted for a less zealous partner. </NOTE>

<Pol Asciak>: Once I was sure that the three of us were alone in that room, the tension that had been building up turned into resentment. There was no evidence that Kempinski was being muscled into being in this unsavory place.
[Pauses] I asked... well, I shouted at him to explain what was going on and what he was doing sitting there with Vannevar. He tried to calm me down. He then introduced the man to his left—only, not as Egon Vannevar, but as Rainforest Kikinda.

<Elevii A. Tarkka ★☆☆>: What?!

<Pol Asciak>: You heard that right. Kempinski explained that Egon Vannevar was the false identity our suspect used to take care of certain kinds of business. As implausible as it might seem, he said, the man sitting next to him really was Kikinda.

<Elevii A. Tarkka ★☆☆>: Wait, how could Kikinda be alive—I mean in a fully human form?

<Pol Asciak>: At the time, I couldn't believe it either. It all felt like a cruel joke. Barely getting up from his chair, Kikinda extended an uncertain hand for me to shake. I slapped it away in anger. How can that asshole be Kikinda, I asked Kempinski. And who the fuck was inside that LUNA if Kikinda never died?

<NOTE> In retrospect, it is clear to me why Kempinski decided to investigate this case. His was not a "hunch" at all. While reviewing Asciak's warehouse video for reasons I cannot fathom, he must have recognized Kikinda. He knew the true identity of "Egon Vannevar" from the beginning. </NOTE>

<Pol Asciak>: Kempinski apologized for not having been completely honest with me. I guess he was still trying to calm me down.
[Speaking to Tarkka] By the way, I mentioned Onfime Mumbi earlier, remember?

<Elevii A. Tarkka ★☆☆>: The *Conduit* champion who allegedly drowned inside the turbotransporter that crashed into the Amundsen Sea?

<Pol Asciak>: The shell in the warehouse video did indeed contain a player, only it was not Kikinda. It was Mumbi.

<Elevii A. Tarkka ★☆☆>: I— I'm not sure I follow...

<Pol Asciak>: Apparently, and unlike what the flight records say, neither Kikinda nor Mumbi was actually inside that transporter when it went down.
And, trust me, at first I couldn't make sense of that either. More than that, I couldn't *accept* what Kempinski was telling

me. Barely in control of my anger, I told him that the two of us were going to have a long talk about this at the station. That is, after we brought this man in.

<Elevii A. Tarkka ★☆☆>: Did Vannevar react at all to hearing that you were going to take him into custody?

<Pol Asciak>: Vannevar... or Kikinda, or whatever his name is, just put his head in his hands. I guess that he, too, couldn't really believe what was happening.

<Elevii A. Tarkka ★☆☆>: Please continue.

<Pol Asciak>: Well, when I began to talk about taking Kikinda into custody, Kempinski stood up in protest. You don't understand, he said, we can't arrest this man. I slammed my fist on the table, asking him what the fuck was wrong with him. Was that not the man who illegally imported a cyborg? A cyborg that should not even exist to begin with?

<NOTE> Here, Asciak was emphasizing the irregularity of the existence of a player cyborg for Onfime Mumbi when, according to the information at their disposal, Mumbi's dead brain should have been lying somewhere at the bottom of the Amundsen Sea. Asciak did not know this at the time, but Mumbi should also not have been reborn as a cyborg because he had never signed a consent form agreeing to the operation. </NOTE>

<Pol Asciak>: Kempinski replied, reasonably, that I was right. Under normal circumstances, taking him in would clearly be what we should do. In this particular case, however, Kempinski argued that the reasons I had listed were exactly why we should *not* arrest this man. [Pauses] At that point, I had had enough. I took out my squeak to read Kikinda his rights. That's when Kempinski grabbed me by the arm.
To stop me, you know. But when he touched me I... I just lost it.

<Merel Asciak>: Pol...

<Pol Asciak>: I—

<Elevii A. Tarkka ★☆☆>: Mister Asciak, would you like to request that we take a break?

<Pol Asciak>: [Shakes his head] No. [Pauses] I turned around and grabbed Kempinski by the collar of his coat. He stuttered something, but I was well past listening to him. I guess he must have tried to free himself...
[Pauses] There was a step behind him, or something. I don't recall. It was dark, and he... he lost his balance.

<NOTE> In the silence that followed, Bakola's camera eyes could be heard whirring as they adjusted their focus. </NOTE>

<Pol Asciak>: I nearly lost my balance, too, and had to let go of him. I managed to steady myself, but Kempinski did not. He fell and hit his head on one of the chairs.
[Pauses] I— I did not mean to hurt him, I swear...We all remained silent for a long while. Asciak was looking down at his own hands. Then he said that there was a lot of blood and that Kempinski wasn't moving. The next thing Asciak did was to put his arms around Kempinski and drag his body out of the room, he said. For some reason, he also specified that he was careful not to step in the expanding pool of blood on the floor.

<Pol Asciak>: The rest of it, you can see for yourself in the recording. Deputy Satia called an emergency medical unit and arrested our suspect.

<Elevii A. Tarkka ★☆☆>: We do indeed have Satia's footage of that. What were you doing while Satia were in the back room with the suspect?

<Pol Asciak>: I... I lay Kempinski down on a table and tried to stop the bleeding with a towel. He barely had a pulse when the emergency unit finally got there.
[Pauses] Well, Mister Young didn't need much of an explanation for why his bar was going to remain closed that evening. I advised him not to leave the sector and let him know that the forensic team would soon be in touch.

<Elevii A. Tarkka ★☆☆>: Did you follow the emergency unit to the hospital?

<Pol Asciak>: I did not. Satia went with them. I walked to the security station.

<NOTE> At this point, my hand buzzed with a squeak notification, but I decided to ignore it for the moment. </NOTE>

<Pol Asciak>: I walked straight into Major Azucena's office, determined to resign and hand in my security badge. As the cool-headed person she is, though, the chief told me to calm down and take a seat instead. Of course, she had heard about what happened, and she said that she would not accept my resignation. At least not as long as I was in such an emotional state. And then she began telling me about her meeting with Kempinski earlier that morning. You know, she clued me in on the bigger picture.

<Elevii A. Tarkka ★☆☆>: I'm afraid I don't know what you're referring to.

<Pol Asciak>: Wait, did the chief not brief you about that part?

<Elevii A. Tarkka ★☆☆>: [Appearing annoyed] I can't say that she did, no.

Merel Asciak raised her eyebrows in reaction to my response.

<Pol Asciak>: I see. I guess that's how she tried to keep a lid on things.

<Elevii A. Tarkka ★☆☆>: [Appearing irritated] What does that mean?

<Pol Asciak>: You know, containing the spread of information and stuff. Don't take it personally, Captain. I was part of the investigation, and I was also in the dark until... well, until it was too late.

<Self ☆>: [Interrupting] Very sorry to interject. Major Azucena is waiting outside in the hallway. She has asked us to notify everyone.

<Pol Asciak>: [Smiles] Well, it looks like you and the boss have a few things to catch up on.

<Elevii A. Tarkka ★☆☆>: I...

<Pol Asciak>: Are we done here, Captain?

<Elevii A. Tarkka ★☆☆>: I... [Appearing confused] I guess we are.

What We Owe the Dead

INVESTIGATION DAY 6 (AFTERNOON)

The Three Matriarchs

August 29 – SS8C

Standing up, Pol Asciak pushed the metal chair toward the wall with the back of his knees. He then gave a slight bow and thanked me for my work, especially for how patient I had been with him. This conclusion brought the hint of a smile to his sister's face. She was still sitting, busily organizing notes and papers into the various compartments of her briefcase.

~~As Pol walked slowly toward the door, I asked Deputy Bakola to let some natural light into the room. The large screen in front of us slowly transitioned back to a large window, causing the homeostatic lighting system to adjust to the sunlight that was then coming into Room B2. Against the sunset sky outside, a handful of swallows drew nervous, imaginary curves between Column C and the central syphon of HOOS-MING ONE. In a matter of days, I thought, these last few birds would also leave the megatower.~~

When she had concluded the organization of her briefcase, Merel stood up and shook my left hand. She apologized if the deposition had not been as smooth as I had hoped it would be. She also informed me that her brother was going to be permanently transferred to another security station. He would be working for Station 79B beginning next week, Merel announced with a smile. Pol stood by the door, waiting for his sister. Regardless of the outcome of my investigation, an internal transfer seemed to me to be a fantastic outcome for Pol Asciak. His job as a security officer in Station 8C was obviously going to become significantly harder and less pleasant once the rest of the staff found out about his role—unintentional as it might have been—in Kempinski's accident. Putting his security experience and skills to the service of a far-off sector—or even a different megatower—sounded like a great prospect, given the circumstances.

Before leaving, Merel also offered some words of gratitude for how I had conducted the deposition and mentioned that she was looking forward to reading my report. Given their involvement in the investigation, it would be their federal right to request a copy of the final document.

<NOTE> Informally, I suggested that she not hold her breath while waiting for the report to arrive: there were still a few depositions to take care of, as well as several hours of footage left to examine. I estimated that it would take at least three weeks before I would be able to submit my report for official review. I was wrong about that, however. Just like I had no say in the decision of how or when to begin this investigation, I ended up not being part of the decision about how or when to close it. Below is a record of what happened instead. In all likelihood, I will have to edit this information out of the final version of the report. </NOTE>

The extract that follows, recorded by Deputy Bakola, took place soon after the Asciaks had left the interview room. The Special Unit and I were taking a break and engaging in small talk while waiting for Major Azucena to join us in the interview room.

File ID: KC07
N.E. 330 – August 29, 12:58
[8C-SU Bakola (6584AR-4)]
(text automatically generated from video)

<Self ☆>: Well, that was something. We mean, that Kikinda thing just came out of nowhere.

<Elevii A. Tarkka ★☆☆>: You can say that again.

<Self ☆>: All right. We found that Vannevar-slash-Kikinda deal most unexpected.

I looked coldly at the Special Unit.

<Self ☆>: What? That was hilarious!

<Elevii A. Tarkka ★☆☆>: [Shakes her head] [Checks her LUNA]

<NOTE> At this point, I was reading the message I had received earlier during the last part of the deposition. As I suspected, it was a squeak from Azucena informing me that she was in the hallway outside and happy to meet with us whenever we were finished. </NOTE>

<Self ☆>: Oh, come on, admit it!

<Elevii A. Tarkka ★☆☆>: [Still checking her LUNA] At the moment, the only thing I'm prepared to admit is that it was unconvincing.
[Turns to Us] I'm talking about Asciak's hazy account of what happened at Clem's.

<Self ☆>: [Relieved] For a moment there, we thought you were criticizing our sense of humor, Captain.

<Elevii A. Tarkka ★☆☆>: [Sarcastically] I wouldn't dare!

<Self ☆>: May we ask you what you found unconvincing about Asciak's deposition? We mean, what if what happened really came down to just a banal mishap?
[We pause] After all, things *can* be simply dumb and tragic accidents. Think of how we ended up in this shell, for example.

<Elevii A. Tarkka ★☆☆>: Is this another one of your jokes, or...

<Self ☆>: Concerning Asciak's testimony, something we could quickly check is the footage captured by the security cameras at Byrgius spaceport.

<Elevii A. Tarkka ★☆☆>: To check for the scene that allegedly involved Kempinski and his mysterious former colleague?

<Self ☆>: Affirmative. We have a date and an approximate time, and it should be easy to determine from which gate the cruiser to HOOS-MING ONE departed. This course of action should corroborate that part of Asciak's deposition. It might not be much, but it would be a start, right?

<Elevii A. Tarkka ★☆☆>: And it may allow us to identify the bearded man, too, in case we need to go down that road. The more I think about it, the more that sounds like a great idea.

<Self ☆>: Why, thank you!

<NOTE> The Special Unit underscored their facetious tone by performing a goofy curtsy. </NOTE>

<Elevii A. Tarkka ★☆☆>: I'll bet you anything, though, that where Kempinski sat at the gate turns out to be a carefully chosen blind spot—a row of seats bafflingly out of reach of all the cameras monitoring the—

I stopped mid-sentence at the sight of Pol Asciak. I was expecting the chief to come in. Instead, Mister Asciak walked back into the interview room with a strange awkwardness. He must have forgotten something, I thought. He offered a forced smile and walked back to his chair. Merel Asciak and Major Azucena made their way into the room soon after, engaged in what appeared to be a cordial chat. The chief closed the door behind her once inside the room. Needless to say, I was puzzled about what was going on.

<Hestia Azucena ★★☆>: Good afternoon, everyone!

<Elevii A. Tarkka ★☆☆>: [Stands up] Major.

<Hestia Azucena ★★☆>: Captain Tarkka. [Nods] I know we had a—how to say—a smaller meeting planned. I hope you don't mind some additional company for a little while.

<NOTE> In the video, you can see me open my mouth as if to say something. Nothing, however, came out. </NOTE>

<Hestia Azucena ★★☆>: And how are we doing today, Deputy?

<Self ☆>: Not too good, Chief. Not good at all, actually.

<Hestia Azucena ★★☆>: [Appearing worried] Hmm?

<Self ☆>: We feel so bad. In fact, that one could say we are just a *shell* of our former selves. [We chuckle]

<Hestia Azucena ★★☆>: [Chuckles]

<Elevii A. Tarkka ★☆☆>: [Inaudible]

The last rays of the setting sun were now entering the room at a slanted angle. The boss was dressed in her uniform, her thick-framed glasses dangling on her chest. She looked at everyone in the room with a smile before starting to speak.

<Hestia Azucena ★★☆>: Okay, everyone, please take a seat and make yourselves comfortable. There is something I'd like to show you, and what more convenient occasion than this, when all of us are already in the same room?

<Elevii A. Tarkka ★☆☆>: [Still standing] I... could I please have a word in private?

<Hestia Azucena ★★☆>: Can't it wait a few minutes, Captain?

<Elevii A. Tarkka ★☆☆>: With all due respect, Major, I have already waited long enough.

<Hestia Azucena ★★☆>: [Stares at Tarkka]

The room fell so silent that the video feed picked up the faint whirring of Bakola's leg actuators as they adjusted their position on the chair.

<Elevii A. Tarkka ★☆☆>: Just to be clear, it's not my

satisfaction with the variety of food options in the vending machine or my housing arrangements that I need to talk about.

<Hestia Azucena ★★☆>: Well, if it's about the Kempinski case, then you can speak freely. We don't need to have a private sidebar for that: everyone in this room is already... how to say, "in the know."

<Elevii A. Tarkka ★☆☆>: Everyone apart from Bakola and me, apparently. Look, my family name is Finnish. It means something like "sharp," which some find ironic, as I tend to be quite blunt.
[Pauses] Major, I want to specifically address your personal involvement in my investigation, and I'm not sure that this is the right context to—

<Hestia Azucena ★★☆>: [Interrupting] [Appearing unperturbed] As I said, if this is about the investigation, you can just go ahead. Just say what you have to say.

<NOTE> I looked at her in silence, trying to understand what kind of game Azucena was playing and whether my role in it was that of a fellow player or a mere pawn. </NOTE>

<Elevii A. Tarkka ★☆☆>: [Stares as Azucena] Very well then.
[Sits down] You intentionally withheld case-relevant information from me.

<Hestia Azucena ★★☆>: Oh...
[Sits down]

<Elevii A. Tarkka ★☆☆>: You omitted crucial details both from the briefing documentation you sent me and from our introductory meeting. I am referring, for example, to the fact that Kempinski knew about Rainn Kikinda's involvement from the very beginning of the Vannevar case. You have known that for about two weeks, since Kempinski initially showed you Asciak's warehouse footage.

<Hestia Azucena ★★☆>: [Purses her lips] You're right that I've known that for some time, of course. In case it makes

it any better, it wasn't until the morning of the 14th that I found out, though.
[Pauses] You see, when Stan originally came into my office with that footage, he didn't inform me about Vannevar's true identity. He was trying to get the investigation off the ground by pitching it as a run-of-the-mill smuggling case.

<Elevii A. Tarkka ★☆☆>: So as something that was too boring for Kempinski to be possibly interested in?

<Hestia Azucena ★★☆>: Exactly, and I was indeed immediately suspicious of his particular interest in this case. I was worried that he was going to get himself into trouble, so I decided to put Inspector Asciak on the case, too.

<NOTE> I imagine that Kempinski must have protested that decision. At the same time, he must have been aware that the overlaps between Asciak's prior investigation and the new one he was starting made the inspector's involvement in Kempinski's new case practically inevitable. </NOTE>

<Elevii A. Tarkka ★☆☆>: And there's more that you've held back from me, Major. Like the fact you never actually officially booked Vannevar.

<Hestia Azucena ★★☆>: [Pauses] Listen, Elevii. Can I call you Elevii?

<Elevii A. Tarkka ★☆☆>: [Appearing unfazed] You let him go as soon as he was brought to the station on August 14th, didn't you? Which is why Vannevar's clumsily created profile still looks pristine: no criminal record or information concerning his arrest.
[Turns to Us] And also why Bakola and I could not schedule an interrogation with him.
[Turns to Azucena] He is not being held in custody, and I think I deserve to know why you hid all these things from me.

<Hestia Azucena ★★☆>: You certainly do, Elevii, which is in fact why I'm here—believe it or not.
[Pauses]
[Talking to herself] Well, where should I begin?

<Elevii A. Tarkka ★☆☆>: Why not begin with what Kempinski told you on August 14th, the day of the accident? What did the two of you talk about when he barged into your office wearing civilian clothes that morning?

<Hestia Azucena ★★☆>: [Takes a deep breath] Okay. On that morning, Stan was as excited as I had ever seen him. When I asked him why he had stormed into my office when he was supposed to be taking the day off, he sat down and gave me the whole story. You know, starting with his acquaintance with Kikinda and finishing with a debriefing of the recent moon mission.

<Elevii A. Tarkka ★☆☆>: [Crosses her arms]

<Hestia Azucena ★★☆>: You see, Stan was convinced that the player inside the warehouse shell was Onfime Mumbi, a retired *Conduit* champion who apparently never signed up to be reborn as a cyborg. Barely containing his excitement, he showed me the automated recognition notification hit on Kikinda that he had received less than an hour earlier.

<Elevii A. Tarkka ★☆☆>: Wait. Are you saying that Kempinski suspected an accountant from the moon of being part of...

<Self ☆>: [Interjecting] A software developer, Captain.

<Elevii A. Tarkka ★☆☆>: Whatever. Did he suspect Kikinda of running a slave trade of sorts?

<NOTE> Here, I was obviously referring to an illicit operation that put players inside cybernetic bodies and forced them to continue playing and/or to become grotesque trophy pets. </NOTE>

<Hestia Azucena ★★☆>: Not quite. Stan thought Kikinda could hack together a shitty false identity on his own. He gave him that much credit. Faking a turbotransporter crash and organizing a secret, illicit rebirth was, however, a scenario of a completely different scale. The kind that requires the participation of an entire organization.

<Elevii A. Tarkka ★☆☆>: Hmm.

<Hestia Azucena ★★☆>: Stan suspected that Kikinda was working for some unsavory people, likely to pay off some kind of debt. As you know, the cyborg of a prominent player can be worth a small fortune.

<Elevii A. Tarkka ★☆☆>: Hold on! If, on the morning of the 14th, Kempinski told you that he suspected the involvement of a criminal organization, why did you consent to his going to face Kikinda on his own?

<Hestia Azucena ★★☆>: First, because his plan was not to raid Kikinda's apartment or to apprehend him. Stan just wanted to talk to him. He was going to try to approach him casually, on the basis of their prior acquaintance.

<Elevii A. Tarkka ★☆☆>: To persuade him to admit to his criminal activities?

<Hestia Azucena ★★☆>: More specifically, to convince him to work with us. To help us take on the larger criminal operation. In exchange for protection, that is.

<Pol Asciak>: [Interjecting] What?! Stan was trying to set up an infiltration operation?

<Hestia Azucena ★★☆>: Yes, that's right. He thought Kikinda would lead us to the rest of the gang. And, for that to work, Vannevar needed to remain free and to continue to operate. That's why I decided not to proceed with Vannevar's arrest, even after Stan's accident.

<Elevii A. Tarkka ★☆☆>: [Speaking to Azucena] And second?

<Hestia Azucena ★★☆>: Second?!

<Elevii A. Tarkka ★☆☆>: Yes, what was the other reason why you decided not to try to stop Kempinski from approaching Kikinda alone?

<Hestia Azucena ★★☆>: Oh, right. Well, knowing Stan, he wouldn't have listened to me anyway, and I saw no point in trying. He wasn't going to let this opportunity slip through his fingers.

<NOTE> Tell me you are an enabler without telling me you are an enabler. </NOTE>

<Elevii A. Tarkka ★☆☆>: [Shakes her head] [Inaudible]

<Hestia Azucena ★★☆>: Try to understand my position. After the accident, security protocol dictated that I had to launch an internal investigation, but my duty to Kempinski and his case simultaneously demanded that I protect Kikinda's cover. That meant, again, that he had to be able to continue to operate as Vannevar, with no record of contact with us.

<Elevii A. Tarkka ★☆☆>: Right, and your way of dealing with that tension was… biding your time by feeding me half-truths to hobble this investigation?

<Hestia Azucena ★★☆>: I'm not saying I'm proud of that decision, but I still believe it was the best I could do at the time.

<NOTE> Rationally, and now with some distance from what happened, I can see the major's point. Pragmatically, she did what she did to avoid compromising a delicate investigation and in the best interest of both her officers. She must have considered breaking the law and wasting my time to be an acceptable trade-off while waiting for the situation to develop. </NOTE>

<Elevii A. Tarkka ★☆☆>: So, what am I supposed to do now? Lie in my report?! Cover your ass and pretend I never knew any of this?

<Hestia Azucena ★★☆>: I'm not asking you to take responsibility for my decisions, Captain.

<Pol Asciak>: [Mumbling] You do you, bub.

<Hestia Azucena ★★☆>: [Speaking to Pol Asciak] What was that?

<Pol Asciak>: [Shakes his head] Don't mind me.

<Hestia Azucena ★★☆>: [Speaking to Tarkka] In response

to your question, Elevii, keep in mind that whatever you write in your report will need to remain classified for the time being. At least for as long as the so-called Vannevar case remains open.

<Pol Asciak>: [Speaking to Azucena] Open?! What do you mean? Who's going to be on the investigation after I'm gone?

<Merel Asciak>: [Interjecting] Is the case going to remain under the authority of Station 8C?

<Hestia Azucena ★★☆>: All right, all right. Calm down, everyone. It would be a lot easier to answer your questions if you would allow me to finish this little show and tell. [Puts on her glasses] Now...
[Speaking to Us] Deputy, would you mind activating the big screen for me, please?

<Self ☆>: Not in the slightest.

As the interrogation room window turned into a screen once again, the room became progressively darker. The automatic lighting system filled the room with the usual diffuse radiance.

<Self ☆>: Anything else we can do for you, Major?

<Hestia Azucena ★★☆>: [Speaking to Us] Actually, yes. You can call Special Unit Deputy Satia and ask them to share their frontal viewpoint. They've been expecting our squeak-call.

<Self ☆>: Squeaking Deputy Satia right now.

Everyone around the table turned to face the screen, which for a while showed nothing but Bakola's squeak interface informing us that the connection was in process. It took a little while for Satia to pick up. When they did, the five of us in the interview room were looking at an extreme close-up of some coarse, pale green fabric.

"Good afternoon, Deputy," Azucena called out.

"Just... just give us a moment, Major. We..." The image on the screen kept tilting and shaking. Some kind of metal struts could occasionally be seen at the edge of the Special Unit's field of vision.

It was hard to tell what was happening on the basis of the visual cues presented on the screen. "Nearly there. Sorry to keep you all waiting," Deputy Satia announced.

As it turns out, the Special Unit were climbing onto a hospital bed, negotiating their way up its metal frame. Once Satia had reached the summit of their ascent, their frontal cameras promptly refocused on what was in front of them. Lying on the bed, awake and alert, was Kempinski. The field deputy was pale and unshaven, and his head and left eye were covered in bandages. He was smiling at the camera. "They can see you now, Stan," we heard Satia say. With a casual tone that added to the surreal feeling of what we were watching, Major Azucena informed us that Kempinski had awoken from his trauma-induced coma yesterday morning. The medical staff had not expected him to wake up so soon—and not necessarily at all—and regarded his spontaneous return to consciousness as a small miracle. "He isn't fully out of the woods," Azucena continued, "but there is reason enough for cautious optimism. He might still lose the eye, though."

Maintaining her nonchalant tone, the chief asked Kempinski how he was feeling and whether he and Satia were alone in the room.

File ID: KC07
N.E. 330 – August 29, 13:22
[8C-SU Bakola (6584AR-4)]
(text automatically generated from video)

<Stanisław Kempinski ☆☆>: I must say that I've had worse days, Hestia.
[Smiles] And, yes, it's only me and Satia here. We can speak freely.

<NOTE> Kempinski's speech seemed a little slower and more slurred than it had been in the other videos I had seen of him, but his statements were clear, overall, and easy to follow except for an intermittent, annoying beeping sound that shrilled in the background every 20 seconds or so. </NOTE>

<Hestia Azucena ★★☆>: Apologies for not having found the time to arrange a way for you to see us.

<Stanisław Kempinski ☆☆>: That's fine. Don't worry about it.

<Hestia Azucena ★★☆>: We're calling from the interview room on Floor B. Five of us are here. Sitting next to me is Pol...

<Stanisław Kempinski ☆☆>: Ah! Howdy, Inspector.

<NOTE> Evidently in shock, Pol Asciak stuttered a quasi-salute in response. The sounds that actually came out of his throat were for the most part incomprehensible. </NOTE>

<Hestia Azucena ★★☆>: Sitting to Pol's left is Merel Asciak, Pol's legal representative. I told you about her yesterday.

<Stanisław Kempinski ☆☆>: Pleasure to meet you, Miss Pol's sister.

<Merel Asciak>: [Appearing confused] L-likewise, Officer.

<Hestia Azucena ★★☆>: Continuing around the room to the left, sitting opposite me are Special Unit Deputy Bakola.

<Self ☆>: Great to have you back, Stan!

<Hestia Azucena ★★☆>: And last but not least is Captain Elevii Tarkka from Sector 78A. Captain Tarkka is in charge of the internal investigation tasked with determining... well, determining what happened to you.

<Stanisław Kempinski ☆☆>: [Nods] Hello, Captain.

<Elevii A. Tarkka ★☆☆>: H-hello.

<Hestia Azucena ★★☆>: Stan, let me begin by thanking you for making the time to talk to us.

<NOTE> Major Azucena must have used that expression out of habit, unthinkingly, as a way to make her interlocutor feel welcome. Her phrasing, in other words, had a social value rather than a functional one. She obviously did not mean to imply that Kempinski had a tightly packed schedule. </NOTE>

<Stanisław Kempinski ☆☆>: [Shrugs slightly] As you can see, I'm not particularly busy at the moment. All I have to keep myself entertained is this small window.

Kempinski made a slight gesture to his right with his bandaged head. Satia followed his cue and looked in the direction of the window. From what I could tell, it was oriented toward the central syphon, overlooking one of the bird sanctuaries.

<Hestia Azucena ★★☆>: Well, yes. Of course. [Adjusting her glasses] Moving on... Stan, would you be so kind as to repeat what you told me yesterday?

<Stanisław Kempinski ☆☆>: That you have no business looking that good at your venerable age?

<Hestia Azucena ★★☆>: You can't stop yourself, you old fool, can you?

<Stanisław Kempinski ☆☆>: [Overacting] What? You still have great legs, and I—

<Hestia Azucena ★★☆>: [Interrupting] I was obviously referring to what you found out about Kikinda. *Diós mío!*

<Stanisław Kempinski ☆☆>: Ah, yes. Case-related stuff. Right.
[Smiles] So, first things first. I'm going to assume that everyone in the room is on the same page concerning who Vannevar actually is now?

<Pol Asciak>: [Interrupting] Hold on a second, Stan. Please.

<Stanisław Kempinski ☆☆>: Is that Pol?

<Pol Asciak>: Yes. Pol here. I... I have something that I want to say.

<Stanisław Kempinski ☆☆>: Is it about the boss being hot for a chick nearing retirement?

Deputy Bakola struggled to contain their delight at Kempinski's rolling banter. In response to their poorly suppressed laugh, Pol shot the Special Unit a sidelong look of disapproval across the table.

<Pol Asciak>: Please, I am being serious.

<Hestia Azucena ★★☆>: You don't need permission to speak, Pol. This is neither a disciplinary hearing nor an official deposition. Just say what you want to say.

<Pol Asciak>: I— I just want Stan to know that I am sorry. I truly am.

<Stanisław Kempinski ☆☆>: [Chokes back a yawn]

<Pol Asciak>: [Takes a deep breath] I'm sorry if I treated... [Shakes his head] *that* I treated you with condescension and for not trusting you. And I'm sorry for getting physical with you that day—for being aggressive and grabbing you... and for what followed. Especially for that. [Pauses] I... have a problem with violence, and I am going to seek help to address my behavior.

<Stanisław Kempinski ☆☆>: Seek help, Pol? Where? In Sector 79?

Merel turned her head abruptly toward Azucena, silently demanding an explanation.

<Pol Asciak>: I...

<Stanisław Kempinski ☆☆>: Listen, Asciak. You're a good man and an excellent investigator. I appreciate your apologies, and what you do with your career and your life really is none of my business. Neither is what your deal is with that girl uptower.

<Merel Asciak>: [Appearing agitated] Hold on! How is any of that relevant to—

<Stanisław Kempinski ☆☆>: [Interrupting] I'm not done, lawyer lady. And you don't need to bare your fangs. You're among friends here.
[Smiles] As a token of my friendship, in fact, here's some

good news for you: I don't intend to press charges against your client.

<Merel Asciak>: [Gasps]

<Stanisław Kempinski ☆☆>: You heard that right, Pol. I'm going to sign a statement that confirms your version of what happened at Clem's. You know, what you said about me somehow... losing my balance... and all the rest. [Pauses] Yup, congratulations. You're off the hook, bub!

<Pol Asciak>: Stan, I—

<Stanisław Kempinski ☆☆>: And so, there was no assault, and there was clearly no murder either. As a matter of fact, here I stand—sort of.

<8C-SU BAKOLA>: What a day we are having!

<Stanisław Kempinski ☆☆>: [Interrupting] Mind you, though, there is a catch. [Coughs] There always is, right? But first let me tell you about Kikinda. After all, I guess that is the reason the boss organized this merry get-together.

<Hestia Azucena ★★☆>: [Appearing relieved] Yes. Yes, it is.

<Stanisław Kempinski ☆☆>: [Clears his throat] All right, I'll try to keep this short and manageable. [Pauses] On the 14th, I went and looked for Kikinda in the slums at the center of the column. I spent some time around the general area where I got the automated recognition alerts. I was hoping our suspect would still be in the surrounding area. You know, buying food or stims, just stretching his legs, whatever. When I finally bumped into him, Kikinda didn't recognize me at first. It had been quite a long time, after all, and I guess the years haven't been gentle with me.

<NOTE> It could be argued that he had not been gentle with the years, either. </NOTE>

<Stanisław Kempinski ☆☆>: [Clears his throat] For a number of reasons that there is no need to get into right

> now, as soon as I saw Kikinda picking up that shell in the video, I suspected he was part of an organized criminal group. And if he really was in a gang, being arrested or having his cover blown would have pretty much meant a death sentence for him.

<NOTE> What Field Deputy Kempinski was alluding to here was the fact that, in those situations, a criminal gang member is often murdered to prevent him or her from collaborating with security or leaking information concerning the group's operations. </NOTE>

> <Stanisław Kempinski ☆☆☆>: And so, since I was working the case with two lovely individuals who would not bend the rules in service of the best outcome, I had to keep his identity to myself.

> <Hestia Azucena ★★☆>: Weren't you going to keep this short?

> <Stanisław Kempinski ☆☆☆>: Yeah, yeah. Now, where was I? [Pauses] So, I was already working in security when I knew Kikinda back on Byrgius.
> [Clears his throat] So I cannot blame him for not being eager to be seen with me. When I asked him to join me for a drink that morning, he quickly said that he was terribly sorry but that he had something or another to do instead.

Kempinski picked up a pink postplastic glass from his bedside table and drank from it, presumably in an attempt to pacify his throat.

> <Stanisław Kempinski ☆☆☆>: When the conversation got to that point, I had no choice but to tell him that I knew he was smuggling cyborg players under a false identity and that I wanted to help him out of this situation.
> Upon hearing that, his expression changed, and the idea of a drink didn't seem so undesirable anymore. I suggested we walk together to a bar just a few minutes away on foot. A small place run by somebody I knew, I told him. A place where we could talk... where there'd be no cameras and no pigs.

> <8C-SU BAKOLA>: *Say what you will about Kempinski, but you cannot accuse him of not being consistent.*

<ELEVII'S LUNA>: *Are you referring to the fact that he is drinking (or is already drunk) in each of the videos we watched, potentially including the present one?*

<Stanisław Kempinski ☆☆>: We started talking as we were walking toward Clem's. Straight away, he confessed that he was working for someone on the moon—a criminal organization, but he only knew his immediate superiors. He also confirmed my suspicions that the player in the LUNA in the warehouse video was indeed the great Onfime Mumbi. [Clears his throat] Their plan was ingenious. Its first step was having Kikinda sign up for the rebirth program. That was roughly a month before the turbotransporter crash.

<Self ☆>: [Interjecting] Perhaps this is an irrelevant detail, but it was more like seven weeks before the crash when Kikinda signed up for the program. At least according to Kikinda's identity profile.

<Stanisław Kempinski ☆☆>: Yeah, well... Anyway, several weeks later, they staged the turbotransporter accident in which Mumbi and Kikinda supposedly died. The criminal organization infiltrated the private company that organized player transport to the Kleff Invitational. I'm saying that because, regardless of what the passenger log for that flight reported, neither Mumbi nor Kikinda was actually on that transporter. At the time, Mumbi was being murdered in a culpably involved medical center on the moon and housed in a LUNA shell against his will.

<Pol Asciak>: Fuck.

<Stanisław Kempinski ☆☆>: Fuck indeed. [Pauses] The organization had likely already found a buyer. Chances are that buyer was some sad fuck living in our sector, or the shell wouldn't have surfaced here.

<Elevii A. Tarkka ★☆☆>: [Whispering] Obviously.

<Stanisław Kempinski ☆☆>: On paper, this buyer would be purchasing a reborn Rainforest Kikinda, a perfectly regular cyborg—a moderately expensive second-division player, authorized for rebirth. A player legally owned by a certain Egon Vannevar. In actuality, they would obtain one of the best *Conduit* players seen in the last decade.

<Hestia Azucena ★★☆>: Awful and, indeed, ingenious.

<Stanisław Kempinski ☆☆>: And that's not all. The really clever part is that, by smuggling the shell instead of going through all the required customs and checks, they can use this trick over and over again. Here's how Kikinda explained it: Mumbi's new owner would request a refund within a few days of receipt, which is their right as a buyer, but no crab would actually be sent back to Vannevar and no refund would be transferred.

<Pol Asciak>: But it would look like they did on official records.

<Stanisław Kempinski ☆☆>: Right. So, once that is done, Vannevar would nominally be back to being the registered owner of a cyborg called Kikinda.

<Pol Asciak>: I see.

<Stanisław Kempinski ☆☆>: The buyer gets a top-notch player at a bargain-basement price, and the criminal organization gets to murder another *Conduit* champion, and start the process again—selling another illegal cyborg as if they were good old Kikinda. A pretty safe and lucrative operation for everyone involved.

<Hestia Azucena ★★☆>: A clever plan, indeed... except that they failed to account for a slow, narcissistic security officer on Earth who would fortuitously recognize Kikinda in the act of smuggling the goods.

<NOTE> Azucena's somewhat vitriolic remark also raises another question about Vannevar and his role: if the organization paying him to carry out this illicit business had access to medical facilities, why didn't they cosmetically alter Kikinda's appearance? Why would they take that chance? Did they simply not have enough time to change his facial features? </NOTE>

<Stanisław Kempinski ☆☆>: [Smiles] I'm the first to admit that we were very lucky. And now we need to make the most of this fortunate hand we were dealt.

<Pol Asciak>: Meaning?

<Stanisław Kempinski ☆☆>: Well, if the criminal organization Kikinda works for can already forge identity profiles, falsify customs records and bank reports, and make indiscriminate use of medical facilities... I mean, how long is it going to be until the next murder? And what's going to happen once they also find a way to forge rebirth authorizations?
[Pauses] What I'm trying to say is that we need to get into the game.

<Hestia Azucena ★★☆>: What he means, more practically, is that the Vannevar case must continue as a covert operation.

<Stanisław Kempinski ☆☆>: [Nods] And that's where the catch is. I'm talking about us, Pol.

<Pol Asciak>: Us?!

<Stanisław Kempinski ☆☆>: As I mentioned, I'm not going to press assault charges for what happened... and I'll sign whatever declaration Hestia and the legal team have cooked up, but I need something from you in exchange. [Clears his throat] I want you to keep working on the Vannevar case. Here, in 8C. With me.

<Hestia Azucena ★★☆>: [Appearing agitated] Stan, that was not part of the deal!

<Stanisław Kempinski ☆☆>: It is now, boss. [Shrugs] We started this together, and I want to end this together. Pol will be off the hook... but only after we solve the Vannevar case. Me, him, and Kikinda as our inside man.

<Pol Asciak>: [Shaking his head in disbelief] But... but why? [Slams both palms down on the table] Why the hell would you even want to work with me? Did your head trauma make you forget that I nearly fucking killed you a week ago?!

Merel Asciak adjusted her sitting posture.

<Stanisław Kempinski ☆☆>: Yeah, well... there's that. But, as much as I might think you're a dick, I also know you're a hell of a security officer. And brave. So you want to know why I want to do this with you? Because it's our duty to stop

> whoever is killing *Conduit* players and selling their corpses into slavery.

Kempinski, evidently uncomfortable with his position on the bed, tried to lift himself up but failed to find a more comfortable position.

> <Stanisław Kempinski ☆☆>: Just like what Grace said on Byrgius. Remember? This is what we owe the dead!

Two days later, in the afternoon, my meeting with Major Azucena finally took place. We met on the main floor of the security station, in Azucena's office. Affable as ever, the chief reported that, after some hesitation and doubt, Pol Asciak had eventually agreed to Kempinski's terms and officially withdrawn his transfer request. Soon, she said, Pol would be reinstated as a security inspector and assigned to work the Vannevar case with Satia. And with Kempinski, of course, once the field deputy was dismissed from the hospital and deemed fit for work.

**** Personal Log, 8/29/330 ****

As promised, Kempinski had signed a written account of the events that unfolded on August 14. That declaration, Azucena told me, confirmed the version of events that Pol Asciak presented during his deposition. Needless to say, I was asked to omit all information regarding their agreement in my report. The chief slid a copy of Kempinski's statement over the desk for my perusal. She commented that Deputy Bakola had already put a digital version of the same declaration in the shared folder dedicated to the case.

Incidentally, Deputy Bakola did not take part in that meeting because they had been assigned to new security tasks earlier that day, following my case's official closure. Azucena took care of everything. The station records concerning what happened that afternoon at Clem's no longer had information gaps or contradictory testimony. To use Kempinski's words, there had been no assault, and clearly no murder either. A banal accident, case closed.

"We won't take up any more of your precious time here, Captain," Azucena said as the meeting was concluding. "You still need to submit your report, of course. Please do that within two weeks. As I have already mentioned, however, the document will remain classified for the time being because of the obvious dependencies between your investigation and... well, let's keep calling it the Vannevar case." I just nodded, feeling—once again—superfluous and alone. Regardless of what I present in the final version of my report (or how much I emphasize the various irregularities that punctuated the process I was tasked with examining), my work will not affect their case anyway.

Before leaving the major's office, I took *Antigone* out of my bag and handed the old, paper book back to her. She shook her head, smiled, and said that I should keep it. Then she hugged me goodbye. That felt pretty weird.

The next morning, I headed home. During a cross-sector check on my way uptower, I livenoted a parting squeak to Bakola, as I did not have the chance to bid them farewell or to thank them in person for their help. I let them know that I was grateful for their support and their kindness throughout the whole process. I also asked them to say goodbye to Captain Kutta for me.

A few minutes later, I received two squeak-messages back from the Special Unit: "It was great working together" and "Everyone here will miss you *pig* time." To their second message, they added a picture of a piglet. Just for good measure, I guess.

****

PART 2

GRACE

("What We Owe the Dead" by Dr. Grace Tizzi. The text appeared in *Cond-Passion Magazine* Vol. 258 [Sept. 330], pp. 17–21, as an installment of Dr. Tizzi's column, "Notes from the Otherground.")

- Notes from the Otherground -

WHAT WE OWE THE DEAD

I was a first-year student at Byrgius University when the first human woman was reborn. For that whole week, the famous video of the cyborg's unsteady walk out of the LUNA research facility looped on every news networks. I remember the conservative media denouncing the rebirth program as state-sanctioned necromancy. To some particularly vocal individuals, cyborgs symbolized the epitome of human hubris: the monstrous proof of our contempt for an alleged "natural order of things." Religious figureheads also went on record condemning technological rebirth as an abomination in the eyes of God (or the gods, depending on their creed). It seemed that no divine beings, however, were powerful or interested enough to stop the production of human–machine hybrids. In the subsequent months and years, half a dozen tech companies followed in LUNA's wake, and increasing numbers of people opted in for participation in rebirth programs.

When I originally came up with the title of this month's column, I had another article in mind. My initial plan did not involve writing about cyborgs. It was supposed to be a piece about the Fleeting, discussing how one untimely visit of those space-faring extraterrestrials continues to affect us to this day. I wanted to talk about how, centuries after the deciphering of their scrolls, these scrolls are still driving the advances in science in many fields closely tied to the survival of our species. The column I had in mind would not have been solely about what we have inherited from our visitors, however. Its focus was to be on what we, as humanity, owe to the Fleeting in return for this inheritance.

When the story of the illicit rebirth of Onfime Mumbi broke in the news a few days ago[1], I knew that my plans for this column needed to change. I had to write a different story. What happened was too big for the *Conduit* community (and, really, for our species in general) to let several weeks pass before addressing it. In the end, I decided to write a column that combines two ideas: this article is both about the duties we have toward those who have long since passed (in this case, the Fleeting) and about our moral obligations to those who, like Onfime Mumbi, have recently died. The result is a longer piece than usual, and I hope it will nonetheless hold your interest.

Needless to say, the conclusion will feature a section about *Conduit*.

Have fun!

. . .

In the words of the Old Era German philosopher Immanuel Kant, the fact that we have duties and obligations toward people who are dead is something that is "as strange as it is undeniable."[2] It is indeed rather odd to feel that we have moral obligations to someone who is no longer alive and cannot be personally harmed by our actions (or lack of action). To clarify what I mean, I ask the reader to think about our immediate predecessors—say, people who lived two or three generations before our own. Preparing for their own death, our ancestors may have expressed certain desires concerning the time after their eventual passing. Those needs and aspirations may have been stated openly ("I want to have a Catholic funeral") or merely implied (as in one's wish to be remembered and cherished once they are gone). Regardless, it should not be particularly controversial to consider fulfilling these desires to be part of our duties to the dead.

---

1. In case you have been living under a slab of moon basalt, a couple of months ago, Mumbi was kidnapped, murdered, reborn, and forced into a cyborg body against his will. This was not a tragic accident or simply an act of cruelty against one of the greatest players of our time. Rather, investigative work led by HOOS-MING ONE (SS8C) revealed it to be part of a human trafficking scheme meant to sell *Conduit* champions as private cyborgs. This was obviously shocking, and particularly so for *Conduit* enthusiasts.

2. Kant, *The Metaphysics of Morals*, Cambridge University Press, O.E. 1996, p. 295.

To be sure, I do not speak here about outlandish demands such as those advanced by Jeremy Bentham, to refer to a notorious case. In his will, the Old Era British social reformer explicitly requested that his embalmed remains continue to attend UCL board meetings for the rest of eternity. I swear I am not making this up. The kind of duties I am talking about, instead, are basic obligations: responsibilities that are practical, reasonable, and rooted in a shared sense of morality. The most obvious and common among such duties are, of course, practices related to respecting the body and the memory of the deceased. To the catalog of such practices, in light of recent events, I propose that we should also add the duty to let the dead remain dead, if that is what an individual wished while they were still alive.[3]

As I mentioned in the introduction to this unusual column, I can still remember the day when the first woman was reborn. I also happen to be old enough to have been alive when the HOOS-MING FOUR syphon megatower was in its final stages of construction. I was only a child then, but I have vivid memories of people despairing that the upper sectors of the Icelandic megatower would never be completed. In response to the widespread metal availability crisis that was challenging the realization of the cooling megasyphon (a crisis that we are still facing today, to some extent), HOOS-MING FOUR launched a now famous droid campaign. Its goal, as every elementary school student knows, was salvaging iron from unsubmerged old buildings and abandoned infrastructure, with truss bridges and railway tracks being among the most obvious scavenging targets. The campaign did not spare even the Eiffel Tower, one of the Old World's most recognizable landmarks. Once the emblem of the grandeur and entrepreneurial *élan* of the French people, the half-sunken, trellised structure was consumed by worker droids in two short weeks.

As I was born into a family of French descent, the undoing of *La Dame de Fer* affected the child version of me profoundly. When its

---

[3]. Conversely, for those who express the desire to be reborn as a cyborg after dying, we should also consider it our moral responsibility to fulfill that wish (provided that they signed up for the program and that the requisite funds are available, of course). Otherwise, each of us has the right to have our brains pulverized together with the rest of our dead body and poured into growth vats to feed the algae.

dismantling was announced, my parents started a protest and filed a formal complaint with the federal authorities. A few thousand individuals who shared our cultural heritage joined mom and dad in contesting HOOS-MING FOUR's decision. My parents claimed that Eiffel's iconic building played a role in shaping and upholding their cultural identity and that it would be disgraceful to see it dismantled when so many insignificant metal structures were still out of the water and available for scavenging. Their complaint was not that the tower's undoing would go against the posthumous desires of some old French engineers. After all, Eiffel's iconic tower was meant to stand only as a temporary showpiece (with a 20-year permit that expired in 1909 O.E.). Rather, my mother and father believed that the destruction of the Eiffel Tower would cause a different, secondary kind of moral damage, which could be labeled as "transcendental." From their perspective, the works and traces left behind by our ancestors are the conditions for us to develop and maintain a certain sense of ourselves (be it cultural, political, sexual, or what have you). The protesters' pleas were, alas, futile, but I hope they show that the dead can also be morally harmed in a way that is indirect, and that some of our obligations toward them are actually things we owe the living.

To summarize, I have highlighted two ways of thinking about our duties to the dead. According to the first perspective, our responsibilities to the dead consist of posthumously fulfilling their aspirations when it is practical and reasonable to do so. The second kind of duty to the dead consists of respecting the work and the memory of our predecessors because of what their traces mean to our contemporaries (and in light of what they might represent for future generations).

Setting aside the matter of his murder—a horrifically immoral act in itself—the forced, illicit rebirth of Onfime Mumbi exemplifies an infringement on the first type of moral commitment to the dead, as he was literally "undeaded" against his will. The defilement of historical monuments like the destruction of the Eiffel Tower or the ransacking of an ancient tomb could be cited, instead, as examples of neglect of the second kind of duty.

My dear friend and colleague Binod Brechter recently argued that human beings tend to prioritize the second kind of responsibility over the first.[4] According to Brechter, this orientation reflects the fact that it has proven historically advantageous to focus on practical matters (i.e., present and upcoming needs) over old promises and distant memories. It is due to valuing our future more than our past—in other words, appreciating that the Eiffel Tower no longer stands.

Based on the two kinds of duties outlined above, I invite the reader to engage in a thought experiment. I am asking you to imagine the following scenario: during a hike, you fortuitously encounter a mysterious hole in the ground. The hole turns out to be the ruin of the entrance to an undiscovered, ancient tomb. Descending into the hole, you find the tomb's interior overgrown and covered with dust, but still containing ornaments and artifacts connected to the burial ritual that took place there. Given these conditions, do you think it would be morally justifiable for you to take those ornaments and artifacts?

In an earlier installment of this column, you may recall that I presented a more-or-less unassailable argument explaining in some depth why ransacking an ancient tomb is a reprehensible action. Now, would that action be ethically viable if it were motivated not by personal gain (e.g., selling these artifacts on the black market) but by a desire to preserve and study the experiences and customs of those who came before us? Would seizing the relics and paraments that adorned the old tomb be okay if you were, say, an archaeologist?

Consider this hypothetical situation through the first ethical lens I introduced—that is, in relation to the posthumous desires of our

---

4. B. Brechter, *New Era, New Ethics: Towards a Contemporary Metaphisics of Morals*, Byrgius University Press, N.E. 327, p. 203.

predecessors. From that perspective, the question of whether an archaeologist could be morally justified in removing these ritual artifacts from the tomb could only be answered negatively. By definition, the people who built the tomb thought of that space as sacred—a structure meant to honor the dead and ensure their transition to an anticipated higher level of existence. It would, thus, be wrong for an archaeologist to violate the ancient tomb and remove the objects it contains, as those actions would disrespect the aspirations of its builders, as well as of the individual (or individuals) buried there.

If we instead adopt the second ethical perspective concerning our duties to the dead, however, the archaeologist removing burial artifacts from the old tomb might not necessarily be perceived as acting immorally. We could in fact interpret their actions as steps toward safeguarding those ancient objects and ensuring that the craftsmanship and the belief system of that old civilization remained relevant to contemporary culture and available to the descendants of the dead themselves.

Given this divergence between the two perspectives, what do you think an archaeologist should do in this situation? Should they respect the implicit wishes of the departed or actively engage in the preservation and study of the ancient remains? How are they to understand what their duties are?

When you think about it, humanity was faced with very similar questions when the Fleeting wreck was discovered in the process of digging the foundations for HOOS-MING ONE. Was it ethically viable to explore their interplanetary vessel and open their mysterious crate? Are we morally justified in translating their ancient scrolls and appropriating their technologies? I believe that even the most conservative of my readers will agree that the manuals found in the Fleeting crate have resulted in a net gain for the human race. The innovations that these scrolls inspired have objectively improved our technical capabilities and boosted our chances of surviving a critical phase of our shared history. The question I aim to address in this article, however, does not involve determining whether the actions of opening the crate and deciphering the extraterrestrial scrolls were beneficial for us. What I would like to establish is whether taking these actions aligned with our duties and responsibilities to the dead (again, in this case, the Fleeting).

As far as we can tell, the reinforced box on the Fleeting ship was intended to preserve materials related to the survival of the crew. If that is in fact the case, then our accessing these scrolls did not clash with any of our visitors' detectable desires.[5] One might even claim that our actions preserved what are possibly the last remaining traces of the Fleeting's existence. From this standpoint, learning their language and appropriating their technological solutions do not appear to be exploitative or unethical practices. On the contrary, such actions could be interpreted as virtuous across the board—benefiting both the Fleeting (indirectly) and the human race (directly).

"Okay, but what about the game of *Conduit*?" you may be asking. "What right did we have to adapt this game to our culture? And are we the bad guys for playing it?"

I propose thinking about this question as follows: we may never know for sure why the *Conduit* scroll ended up in that reinforced crate. We also may never find out whether the Fleeting invented *Manifold Passage* (my preferred translation of the game's name) or whether they also inherited this game from an older culture. All we can say for sure is that we owe the survival of our species to a civilization that reached planet Earth from an imponderable distance millions of years ago.

Some claim that *Conduit* is simply a medium and that, like other media, it is characterized by specific functions and qualities. The

---

5. I must emphasize, however, that taking and translating these scrolls did align with our own desires to know more about the Fleeting and their creations.

6. See, e.g., O'Konnor, K. 321, "Brain Remapping and Cognitive Shifts in Duplicate *Conduit* Players: A Transversal Study" in *Cyberpsychology, Behavior, and Social Networking*, n. 421 (2), pp. 429–435.

Fleeting game encourages certain worldviews and behaviors while inhibiting others. Research shows that *Conduit* causes detectable transformations in its players, especially their use of language and their political inclinations.[6] It definitely changed the way I think about the world. In this sense, as I have argued elsewhere,[7] the game might be better understood as a transformative technology (a "technology-of-the-self") rather than just a complicated pastime.

As a medium, *Conduit* was not something that we could understand or use immediately. To be able to play, we had to adapt the game to our socio-technical situation so that it referred to ideas to which we could relate, rather than the obscure alien metaphors and references that haunt the Fleeting version. The process of its cultural translation was neither easy nor short, as you certainly know, but there is no doubt in my mind that it was the right thing to do: tailoring the game to our needs made *Conduit* into a culturally relevant practice and an active way for us to honor the memory of the Fleeting.

To be sure, *Conduit* is clearly more than just a medium for play and communication. Like old books or cyborg shells, it is also a technology that was purposefully designed to keep something alive. It is a ludic machine that contains and promotes specific values and procedures about how to envisage and shape our collective future. What I want to argue, to conclude this article, is that preserving and adapting Fleeting knowledge is not our only option for carrying forward the torch of our long-gone extraterrestrial visitors. We are also realizing this greater task every day by using their technologies and playing their game. We are doing it by becoming Fleeting ourselves, one cyborg at a time, one *Conduit* match after another.

> What do you think about this month's topic? Reach out to Prof. Grace Tizzi using the form below and, who knows, your name might appear in the next installments of "Notes from the Otherground."

---

7. I am specifically referencing my November 328 column, "A *Conduit* for Thought" (in Cond-Passion Magazine n. 236, pp. 15–17), but I also raised the same point in *The Conduit Philology Handbook* (Byrgius University Press, N.E. 320) and more recently in *Across the Deep: A Poetic History of the Game of Conduit* (Set Margins' Press, forthcoming).

PART 3

STEFANO

AFTERWORD BY THE AUTHOR

"This book does not go anywhere," commented one of my early readers. "It feels like a rollercoaster ride where the train remains perfectly still and it's the track that moves around instead." I smiled and nodded, finding the analogy not only very amusing, but also very fitting. *What We Owe the Dead* is indeed a mystery novel with no mystery, or—as someone else described it—a special kind of detective story, one that follows the wrong detective.

I wrote *What We Owe the Dead* while also working my day job as an academic. I didn't do it with the sole purpose of keeping myself off the streets—to channel our own Grace Tizzi's Chapter 8 (INVESTIGATION DAY 5 [Afternoon]) explanation of her career choices. As I see it, experimental works like this one (and like my philosophical videogames) are contiguous with my academic output disseminated through more traditional outlets. As I see it, these less traditional outputs are the portion of my intellectual work that is more likely to have an impact on society.

Like my previous experimental novella (*The Clouds*, published in 2023 by Routledge), the book you are holding is an attempt to combine theory and fiction. It is, in other words, an attempt to breathe new life into specific philosophical questions and ideas. The afterword I wrote for *The Clouds* criticized the often-unquestioned institutional paradigm according to which "doing scholarly work" means producing specific kinds of theoretical manuscripts (the journal article, the academic book review, and so on). I am not going to repeat that argument here, but it should be evident that *What We Owe the Dead* sprouted from that same cerebral soil. The present book is similarly rooted in the belief that works of fiction—in its various forms, including interactive ones—can facilitate a number of processes related to intuition, inference, and empathy, and that those processes are very valuable when we try to communicate ideas (on this theme, see also Calvino 1967; Pezzano & Gualeni 2025). On top of an opportunity to rattle my audience, then, writing novels and making videogames are ways for me to put some "flesh" on philosophical abstractions—and hopefully enough of it to allow those ideas to crawl out of academic repositories, leave research institutions, and meet with larger and broader audiences.

Whereas *The Clouds* is an existential reflection on the simulation hypothesis (the possibility that we are living within an artificial subset of reality), *What We Owe the Dead* focuses on the survival of the human race and our duties to our predecessors. Despite the differences in genre, tone, and structure, the plots of both books revolve around games. Games are particularly central to *What We Owe the Dead*, where a game features as a narrative device that raises some extraordinary questions about transformative experiences and the transmission of values. As you may already know, the idea that games and playfulness are foundational elements for how we function both at the individual level and as social creatures has an extensive history in anthropology, as well as in game studies. As early as 1939, in his book *Homo Ludens: A Study of the Play-Element in Culture*, Dutch historian Johan Huizinga qualified the human being as an inherently playful creature and insisted that civilization "arises in and as play, and never leaves it" (1955, p. 55). In a similar vein, Canadian media theorist Marshall McLuhan observed that "[t]he games of a people reveal a great deal about them. Games are a sort of artificial paradise like Disneyland, or some Utopian vision by which we interpret and complete the meaning of our daily lives" (1966, p. 210).

Studying the games we play as communicative and transformative artifacts is a well-established perspective in game and media studies. Similarly uncontroversial is the idea that games cannot be fully understood apart from the socio-technical contexts from which they arose. In our recent book, *Fictional Games* (published in 2022 by Bloomsbury), for example, Riccardo Fassone and I specifically examine games that exist exclusively as a part of a world of fiction. In the book, we show that fictional games often rely on familiar forms of playfulness and tend to replicate—in distilled, controlled forms—the values and aspirations that characterize the (fictional) culture in which they are produced and played. Mirroring inclinations and traits of their socio-technical milieu is, however, not the only narrative function of fictional games. They may also promote social change within their fictional worlds and function as transformative technologies. Syndrome, the counter-hegemonic fictional board game described by Philip K. Dick in his 1959 short story, "War Game," is a clear example of this subversive use of a fictional game. In "War Game," Syndrome is a Monopoly-inspired game designed by the economically exploited

Ganymedeans to be played on Earth, the home of their oppressors. As playable propaganda, Syndrome promotes non-colonial and non-consumerist player behaviors, leading—as the finale of the story suggests—to a gradual shift in the Terrans' capitalist mindset (Gualeni & Fassone 2022, p. 94). Ken MacLeod's 2011 novel, *The Restoration Game*, is another interesting and similar case where an online multiplayer game becomes the ideological and organizational linchpin of a social revolution.

In a nutshell, two of the main literary functions of fictional games are, first, manifesting trends and tensions that characterize their (fictional) socio-technical context and, second, contributing to subverting the status quo of a certain fictional world.

Central to the plot of *What We Owe the Dead* is a game of extraterrestrial origin derived from a scroll written in an alien language that human beings interpreted as instructions and rules to play. From the vague and partial descriptions found in the book, we know that the alien game called *Duplicate Conduit* (or "Manifold Passage") features playing cards grouped in thematic suits and at least two kinds of boards. For all we know, the alien game may not have originally been designed as a game at all, but rather a tool for organizing social discussions and making collective decisions.

In terms of its narrative uses in *What We Owe the Dead*, the game of *Conduit* combines the two functions outlined above. The game allegedly distills the essence of an alien culture that made contact with our planet millions of years ago. In this first narrative role, *Conduit* is possibly the last, dying ember of an ancient civilization—something that humans accidentally found and decided to rekindle. However, the game is also something that our fictional descendants modified and adapted to fit their needs and cultural referents. In this second narrative use, *Conduit* is at once both something they discovered and something they designed. In the story, learning to play the game appears to have detectable cognitive and ideological effects on human beings, leading to transformations in how they talk, think, and act. In this light— quoting from Grace Tizzi's (fictional) column—*Conduit* might thus be "better understood as a transformative technology [...] rather than just a complicated pastime" (p. 191).

What We Owe the Dead is not only about games. In a loose sense, the novel itself is a sort of game. In a 1985 essay, "The Detective Story: A Case Study of Games in Literature," philosopher and play theorist Bernard Suits proposes a small taxonomy of ways in which a literary work can "correctly"—that is, non-metaphorically—be considered a game (1985, p. 200). The idea that authors can institute a playful challenge to the reader through a work of fiction (a detective novel in particular) has an intellectual history that can be traced back at least to S.S. Van Dine's claim that "the detective story is a game. It is more – it is a sporting event" (1928, p. 27). Within the same scholarly tradition, Peter Hutchinson wrote on the topic of literary play, encompassing both playful writing and the possibility of a ludic relationship between the author and the reader. In his 1983 text, *Games Authors Play*, Hutchinson suggests that "a literary game may be seen as any *playful*, self-conscious, and extended means by which an author stimulates his reader to deduce or to speculate, by which he encourages him to see a relationship between different parts of the text, or between the text and something extraneous to it" (1983, p. 14).

Interestingly, none of these prior authors has advanced claims regarding whether we should understand playfulness as a catalyst to speculative endeavors or whether speculation can itself be considered an inherently ludic pursuit. In any case, I believe it is rather obvious that *What We Owe the Dead* was written with ludic and speculative intentions. Through various kinds of playful deceit, my book is intended to invite the reader to reflect on a number of themes that can be considered to be of philosophical interest. This includes the idea of how our conception of privacy and mortality might change in relation to our growing dependence on technology. It also refers to the questions that the book recurrently asks concerning the personhood of cybernetic beings.

I hope that this playful book—like the game of *Conduit*—will also be a tool for thinking for the reader, and not just a complicated pastime.

ACKNOWLEDGMENTS

Producing a book, at least in the way I do it, is not a lonely pursuit. What I am getting at is that, rather than taking a single fool to put together *What We Owe the Dead*, it took a whole village of fools. I want to use these last paragraphs to thank the foolish people who dedicated their time and attention to this weird literary project.

I am grateful to Nele Van de Mosselaer, Aphrodite Andreou, and Jennifer B. Barrett for their unflappable support, their insightful criticism and feedback. To these readers and others who visited this text in its rickety, formative stages, I am both sorry for putting you through it and thankful for your critical notes and helpful comments. For these contributions, I am additionally grateful to—in no particular order—Daniele Giardini, Susana Tosca, Riccardo Fassone, Valentina Romanzi, Giacomo Pezzano, Johanna Pirker, Rebecca Portelli, Dom Ford, Robin Longobardi Zingarelli, and Chris E. Hekman.

My gratitude also goes to Freek Lomme (Set Margins' press). His open-mindedness and curiosity about this literary experiment helped this book along, starting from its very early stages.

Finally, I would like to thank the University of Malta and the Institute of Digital Games for granting me the time and the resources to pursue creative projects and philosophical reveries such as this one.

July 29, 2024

WORKS CITED

Calvino, I. 1967. "Philosophy and Literature," *Times Literary Supplement*, September 28, 1967.

Dick, P.K. [1959] 2002, "War Game," in *The Minority Report and Other Classic Stories*, New York, NY: Kensington Publishing, loc. 3913–4283.

Huizinga, J. [1938] 1955, *Homo Ludens: A Study of the Play-Element in Culture*, Boston, MA: Beacon Press.

Hutchinson, P. 1983. *Games Authors Play*, London, UK: Methuen.

Gualeni, S. 2023. *The Clouds: An Experiment in Theory-Fiction*, New York, NY: Routledge.

Gualeni, S. & Fassone, R. 2022. *Fictional Games*: A Philosophy of Worldbuilding and Imaginary Play, New York, NY: Bloomsbury.

MacLeod, K. 2011, The Restoration Game, Amherst, NY: Pyr.

McLuhan, M. 1966 [1964]. *Understanding Media: The Extension of Man*. New York, NY: Signet Books.

Pezzano, G. & Gualeni, S. 2025. "How to Do Philosophy with Sci-Fiction: A Case of Hybrid Textuality," *Filosofia*, 69 (1), 249-264.

Suits, B. 1985. "The Detective Story: A Case Study of Games in Literature," Canadian.

Review of Comparative Literature / Revue Canadienne de Littérature Comparée, 12 (2), 200-219.

Van Dine, S.S. 1928. "Twenty Rules for Writing Detective Stories," *American Magazine*, September 1928, 26–30.

Set Margins' #49

What We Owe the Dead

Stefano Gualeni

ISBN: 978-90-834993-4-5

Contributing artists: Daniele Giardini

Graphic design: Benedetta Ferrari

Font: Alpina Standard by Grilli Type

© Stefano Gualeni

First edition, 2025

Set Margins'

www.setmargins.press